THE BOSS

NEW YORK TIMES AND USA TODAY BESTSELLING AUTHOR
MELANIE MORELAND

Dear Reader,

Thank you for selecting The Boss to read. Be sure to sign up for my newsletter for up to date information on new releases, exclusive content and sales. You can find the form here: https://bit.ly/MMorelandNewsletter

Before you sign up, add melanie@melaniemoreland.com to your contacts to make sure the email comes right to your inbox!
Always fun - never spam!

My books are available in paperback and audiobook! You can see all my books available and upcoming preorders at my website.

The Perfect Recipe For **LOVE**
xoxo,
Melanie

The Boss by Melanie Moreland
Copyright © 2021 Moreland Books Inc.
Copyright #1185927
ISBN Ebook 978-1-988610-66-5
Paperback 978-1-988610-67-2/978-1-988610-69-6
All rights reserved

MORELAND
BOOKS INC.

Edited by Lisa Hollett of Silently Correcting Your Grammar
Cover design by Karen Hulseman, Feed Your Dreams Designs
Cover Photography by Wander Aguilar Photography
Cover Model Andrew Biernat
Cover content is for illustrative purposes only and any person depicted
on the cover is a model.

If you are reading this,
then this book is for you.
Thanks for coming along for the ride.

CHAPTER ONE

Evelyn

I raced along the street, tears streaming down my cheeks. The salt stung the abrasions, but I didn't stop to wipe them away. I had to get away—as far away as possible. My head ached from the blow I had taken earlier, and my legs were tired from running, but I kept going.

I stuck to the shadows, pulling my jacket around me, burying my face into my scarf. My pocket contained the only thing I had grabbed before I fled. My small wallet and the five hundred dollars I had snuck from his jacket. I had nothing else with me.

A busy intersection was coming up ahead of me. I didn't want to take the chance of being seen under the bright lights. Having no other choice, I cut down a dark alley. The exact kind of alley a girl was warned to avoid all her life. But, at that point, it didn't matter anymore. If someone grabbed me, they couldn't do any worse than *he* had. If I stayed, I was dead, and I had decided I would rather die running than stay and let him finish me off.

I heard shouts, and my chest tightened. I started to run faster, not caring where I was headed. I ran until I was breathless, from alley to alley, until there were no sounds except my muffled heartbeats.

Leaning against a crumbling brick wall, I tried to catch my breath and let my heart slow down. My vision was clouded, and I had to blink several times to clear it. I tucked my trembling hands under my arms, unsure if I was shaking from the cold or fear. I looked around, no clue where I had ended up. I peeked around the corner at the deserted streets. The neighborhood was industrial, the buildings a mixture of run-down businesses and closed, boarded-up warehouses.

I inhaled a shaky breath, pushing my hair off my face. I winced when my fingers met my forehead, and drawing them back, I saw they were wet with blood. More tears ran down my face. Unsure what to do, I began to walk, trying to gather my thoughts. I couldn't go to a hotel since a credit card would be required. He would trace it. I needed a cheap motel that would take cash and ask no questions. I glanced around—it was the sort of area I might find one, but it had to be soon. My legs began to shake, and the pain in my head increased. I didn't want to risk being out in the open any longer than I had to be.

A car drove by slowly, and my panic returned. It wasn't him, but the sight of it unnerved me, the speed making me wary. I slowed my footsteps, and when the car stopped a few blocks ahead and sat with the engine running, my heart stuttered. There was a narrow break between the buildings, and taking advantage of the sudden escape route, I slipped between them. It was dark, and I used my hand to trace along the wall. I encountered a door handle, and when it turned, I was shocked that it worked. The door creaked in the small passage. I could hear the car that had frightened me coming back, and quickly, I slipped through the door, shutting it behind me.

The air was damp and musty, with mildew and dust tickling my nose. I was shrouded in darkness and eerie silence. I could hear voices outside. Fumbling, I found the lock on the door and pressed it. I held my breath, my panic ramping higher as the voices came closer. The handle jiggled, the lock preventing it from opening. I prayed it would hold, my gaze locked on the dull metal.

"Are you sure she came down here?"

"I thought so. Fuck, who cares, man. We can find another piece of tail."

The voices drifted away, and the car drove off, the sound of the engine fading away. I shuddered, holding my throbbing head. They weren't looking for me, specifically, but I was still grateful for the door I had found. Relief made me even weaker, and for a moment, I had to lean on the damp wall, trying to summon my waning strength.

A few moments passed, and I knew I had to decide what to do now. Leave the way I came in and keep walking aimlessly, or explore what might be a place I could sit and rest for a while and figure out my next move—as limited as my choices were.

Cautiously, I walked forward, coming to another closed door. The shaking in my legs was getting worse, and I hoped to find a place to sit aside from the floor. I wasn't sure I would be able to get up if that was where I ended up. I pushed the door open, peeking around the edge, then entered a large room. From what I could see from the partially boarded-up windows, I was in a deserted warehouse. The dim light helped, and I investigated until I found a glassed-in office that contained some old furniture. Some of the panes were still intact, and they were thick with grime. The rest of the panels lay in shards on the floor. I carefully skirted the glass and sat down behind a timeworn desk. The chair was hard, cold, and damp, but it was big enough for me to curl up in. I drew up my shaking legs, wrapped my arms around my knees, and rested my head on them. I drew in a quivering breath, the feeling of gratefulness for a deserted building and a rickety old chair overwhelming me. The damp, musty smell invaded my senses, the lingering decay reminding me of the basement closet Blaine liked to lock me in on occasion.

The tears restarted, and I let them flow. My sobs were choked and deep, and the ache in my head intensified. My body was a mass of quivering limbs as the last of the adrenaline rush I had been experiencing evaporated, leaving me spent.

How had my life come to this?

The blackness began to gather, and I fought it. I had a feeling if I succumbed, I wouldn't wake up. But it was useless, and gradually, the world dimmed.

I swam to consciousness, my head spinning. I was nauseated and cold, my limbs stiff and painful. I didn't move but stared through the dirty glass, confused. The large room I had wandered through before was lit up, and a group of men stood with their backs toward me, arguing. They flung their arms around, gestured with their hands, and their voices were angry.

Carefully, I eased the chair back as far as I could into the shadows. The little office I was in was still dark, and I didn't think they could see me, but I wasn't taking any chances. One of the missing glass panes was at eye level, and from this angle, I had a clear view of them. Alarm ran along my nerves, telling me I needed to stay silent. Whatever they were doing here was not something I should be seeing.

There were four tall men, all in black coats. One of them towered over the rest. They moved, and I saw another two people. They were sitting on the floor, beaten and bleeding, tied with their backs pressed together.

I shrank back, my terror taking on new proportions. My teeth began to chatter, and I slapped my hand over my mouth to silence the noise. I had to bite down on my lip as well, and I wrapped my free arm around my knees to try to stop the tremors. I heard the loud slam of a door, and another man strode into the room. He was tall, slender, with broad shoulders, his black overcoat long and swaying around him as he walked. He moved with intent, his shoulders taut, his stride fast. His deep brown hair was long, brushing his collar and slicked off his forehead. His face was sharp angles, a tight beard hugging the curves of his face, framing his mouth. His gaze was intense and furious. He commanded the notice of all the men in the room. They stood taller, their shoulders back—almost at attention. They moved to form a wide circle around the people on the floor. He joined them, sneering at the men who were tied up and helpless. He was facing me, his hatred a living, breathing entity emanating from him.

A barrage of words in a language I didn't understand came from his mouth. He raged, his voice echoing in the empty room. More than once, he slapped the helpless prisoners, screaming in their faces. His leather gloves shone in the dim light, blood-red against black, wet and dripping. My stomach lurched at the sight of it, and I pressed my hand harder to my lips.

He stepped back, his face dark, evil, and twisted. He was like an avenging angel—straight from hell. He held out his hand, and one of the men placed a gun in it.

He stared, cold and ruthless, then he nodded. The group of men drew their guns and aimed.

I pressed my hand over my mouth so hard, I felt my lip split trying to hold in my scream, knowing what I was about to witness and unable to look away.

"Burn in hell," he spat.

Gunshots rang out.

The men on the floor jerked, their bodies arched and flailed, then slumped. Blood ran, crimson and thick.

I couldn't control myself. I twitched so hard, the chair moved, hitting the wall with a low thump. I lurched forward, emptying the meager contents of my stomach onto the floor, panting and gasping for air. I grasped the arms of the chair so hard, my knuckles protested. My head swam from the sudden movement. I heard more cursing and rushed footsteps in my direction, but I knew I was trapped.

"What the fuck?" a low voice growled as rough hands gripped my arms, forcing me upright.

I looked up, meeting a pair of brown eyes. They widened then narrowed, brimming with fury. Up close, his face was beautiful—the sort of beauty that easily distorted into fierce malevolence. A devil in disguise.

"Who the *fuck* are you?"

His face wavered in my gaze. There wasn't enough oxygen in the room. It tilted, becoming dim and distorted.

"No one," I whispered, before the world went dark.

CHAPTER TWO

Evelyn

I woke to stinging on my cheeks. I was back in the chair, pushed behind the desk. The devil stood over me, his fingers flicking at my skin. I whimpered, and he hunched lower, his eyes black with rage.

"Awake now?"

I nodded, but the movement made my head hurt. My entire body ached, my muscles spasming with terror. Whimpering, I held my head in my shaking hands.

"Look at me," he commanded.

I lifted my head, the effort causing more tears to pour down my cheeks.

He studied my face before speaking.

"What are you doing here? How did you get into this fucking building?"

I cleared my throat. "It–it was an accident. I got scared, and the door was open by the alley."

"Scared of what?"

"I thought someone was coming after me."

He studied me with narrowed eyes. "Looks like they already did."

More tears leaked from the corners of my eyes. "That was someone else—that was what I was running from."

He crossed his arms, his voice vehement. "You made a mistake coming here."

I hung my head, too exhausted to hold it up. "Please," I whispered, knowing it was useless.

"You saw something you shouldn't have."

"Nothing. I saw nothing," I lied.

He laughed, cruel and low. "You're a lousy liar."

I forced myself to lift my head. "I won't say anything. No one will know. *Please* let me go."

"I can't do that."

The tallest man appeared in the doorway. "Boss? You need help?"

"No. Clean up the mess. Dispose of it."

The tall man stepped forward, laying a gun on the desk.

I started shaking harder, long shudders running down my spine and racking my body. "Please…" I begged, my voice faltering.

"What?" the devil asked.

"Make it fast, please. And let me shut my eyes." My voice wavered as more tears slipped down my cheeks. "There's money in my pocket. Could you drop it at a shelter or something?"

"You assume I'm going to kill you."

I nodded. "To shut me up."

"Yet you're asking for a favor. To help someone else. Not begging for your life."

I didn't know how to tell him my life was over anyway. Blaine would find me and kill me in some fashion. And he'd do it slowly. At least this way, it would be quick. But I didn't respond. I was too tired. I shook my head.

There was silence for a moment. "I don't do errands," he said.

"Maybe one of your men?"

"Why would a dead woman care where her money went?"

A sob burst from my chest. Without thinking, I gripped his arm, the material of his overcoat thick and soft under my fingers. "Please. I'm begging you."

"Now you're begging for your life?"

"No. Begging you to show some mercy and give the money to a place that needs it. You don't need it. But it could help someone like me." I reached my hand into my pocket and pushed the wad of cash into his hand.

He stared, his gaze moving between the cash and my other hand gripping his coat.

"I don't like to be touched."

I pulled back my hand. "I'm sorry."

He took the cash. "Where did you get this money?"

"I stole it."

His eyebrows rose in question. "You *stole* it?"

"Yes."

Movement caught my eye, and I watched, horrified, as the men in the other room rolled the dead bodies into large tarps. I hadn't noticed the canvas on the floor until now. Once the bodies were moved, there would be no trace of them anymore.

I wondered if they had another tarp for my body.

A whimper escaped, and my shaking intensified. My body felt as if it had been shocked, and I had no control over the constant jerks and spasms.

"Don't look at them. Look at me," he ordered.

I snapped my gaze back to his.

"What is your name?"

"It doesn't matter. No one will miss me."

"I *asked* you your name."

"Evelyn."

"Who did this to you?"

Why was he toying with me? Why didn't he just kill me?

"Does it really matter?"

He bent, bringing his face close to mine. "You, *Evelyn*, are trying my patience. You need to learn something. If I ask a question, you answer. If I say do something, you do it. You understand?"

"Y–yes," I breathed out, trying to control the shudders and failing.

"Who did this to you?"

"His name is Blaine."

"Is Blaine your husband?"

I felt a flash of anger. "Why? If he was, does that give him the right?"

He narrowed his eyes, the slits glittering, livid and black in the muted light. "No."

I slumped forward. "No, he isn't. He was my boyfriend. He started beating me after my dad died."

"When was that?"

"S–six months ago," I choked out.

"Did your father like this man?""

I didn't understand his line of questioning or why he cared.

"No. He didn't."

He rubbed his chin. "Your father was a smart man."

"Yes," I whispered.

"Tell me your story."

I wanted to scream at him to stop putting off the inevitable. My story didn't matter anymore. But recalling his warning, I kept that to myself. Swallowing around the painful lump in my throat, I spoke. "My dad got sick, and I left work to look after him. When he died, Blaine insisted I move in with him until I found a job, and that was when it started. We moved, and I didn't know a soul. I had no one to turn to. It's been getting worse. He always apologized and promised not to do it again. Then a month ago, it stopped. I thought he had changed. He brought me from Alberta here to Toronto on a business trip. Except, when we got here, I found out it wasn't a...*business* trip."

"What was it?"

I shut my eyes as the tears flowed again. "He had planned to take me to some sort of party. Sh—sharing me with other men. He'd stopped beating me so I wouldn't be so bruised. When I found out, I tried to leave. He got angry and lost it." I wiped at my cheeks, knowing tears were useless. "He punched me, threw me against a table. I hit my head and fell to the floor. I pretended to be unconscious. He left me there in the hotel room and went to get a drink downstairs. I knew when he came back, he was going to start again. I ran."

"After you took his money."

"I—I thought at least I deserved that. I had nothing else left. I needed some money to find a place to stay."

"And you ended up here."

That was all he said. When I opened my eyes, he was staring at me. There was an odd expression on his face. He leaned against the side of the old desk, his arms crossed.

"What hotel?"

I wanted to ask him why he cared, but I held back those words. "The Conrad."

One of his men walked into the room. "It's done, Boss. Vince is taking out the garbage."

The devil stood. "Fine."

"You want me to handle this?" He nodded toward me.

The boss didn't say anything. He regarded me with his dark eyes, silent and watchful.

"I'd be happy to take her elsewhere and handle it. I'd *enjoy* handling her, if you get my drift," his man added, leering at me. "An added bonus for a job well done tonight."

It happened so fast. My horror grew, knowing what was about to happen. My life would end tonight, but before it did, I would be subjected to even more pain and humiliation. The devil spun on his heel, momentarily distracted, cursing and shouting. With strength I didn't know I still possessed, I lunged out of the chair, grabbed the gun on the desk, and pushed it up under my chin.

I backed away, my hand shaking, the cold metal of the gun pressing into my skin.

The men froze, and the boss stepped forward, meeting my eyes.

"Give me the gun, Evelyn."

"No," I rasped out. "I wouldn't let Blaine, and I won't let you give me away like some piece of trash."

He moved toward me, his voice commanding and lethal. "Give me the *goddamn* gun."

I cocked the trigger, and he stopped.

"No. At least this way, I'm in control."

"You don't have to do this—you don't *want* to do this."

I barked out a laugh. "Why? So you get the pleasure? At least I get to deny you that much."

"Evelyn," he warned.

"I'm going to die tonight. I have nothing left. At least I can do it myself." I met his eyes. "Please give the money to someone who needs it."

He nodded, holding up his hands. I slammed my eyes shut and pushed harder, the gun digging into my skin.

With a final shuddering breath, I pulled the trigger.

CHAPTER THREE

Matteo

I saw the determination in her eyes. Despite the tears and redness surrounding them, they were lovely. Even in the dim light, they were luminous, showing her emotions clearly. There was nothing I could do but wait and pray. If I tried to tackle her, more than one person could die. I couldn't talk to her—she wouldn't listen. So, all I *could* do was wait and pray.

Pray the fucking chamber that had advanced didn't contain a bullet. The revolver should only have three bullets in it, if my men had done as I instructed.

And they always did.

"*Not her.*" That was the odd thought that ran through my head as I stared.

I shouldn't care. It would save me a lot of trouble, but I didn't want her to die.

And I did care. There was something infinitely appealing about this small woman. She was in dire need —that much was obvious. The strangest thing was, I had the insane desire to help her with that need. I braced myself for what was about to happen, silently imploring God that her bravery would be for nothing.

The sounds of the trigger and striking metal were loud in the room, but there was no bullet. I had no time to be grateful as I lunged forward and grabbed the gun away from Evelyn, hauling her tense form back to my body. A rush of relief hit me unexpectedly, and I held her trembling body close.

Frank shook his head. "Stupid bitch. You should have let her die, Boss. I would have." Then he laughed menacingly. "But at least I can still fuck around with her."

Evelyn hadn't moved. She hadn't made a sound since the gun failed to give her what she wanted. Death. But when Frank spoke, her trembling turned into quakes. Long, violent convulsions racked her tiny frame. She was beyond petrified, yet she didn't struggle against my hold.

Despite her fragile appearance, she was strong. Stronger than she knew.

I stared at Frank, my loathing of him growing every passing second. His time was up. What I planned to happen later was happening *now*.

"Marcus," I called.

He appeared.

"Bring me the package."

"Boss?"

"*Now.*"

I moved forward, pushing Evelyn down into the wooden chair where I had first discovered her. "You will sit there and not move. Do you understand? You will remain in that fucking chair no matter what happens next."

Only her terrified, shortened breathing answered me.

I faced Frank, who was watching me with a bored, insolent look on his face.

That would be changing soon.

I heard a commotion from the other room as Marcus returned with the "*package*." He dragged in a highly angry and vocal Carly. She twisted and clawed at him, cursing and hurling obscenities. He flung her on the floor, brushing off his sleeves, wiping off the blood from where her fingernails found purchase on his cheek.

"Bitch," he muttered as he moved away.

Frank rushed past me, snarling.

"What the fuck are you doing?" he shouted to Marcus.

He kneeled beside Carly, whispering—no doubt telling her to let him do the talking.

I checked the gun, and once satisfied, I cast a final warning look at Evelyn. "Don't move."

She stared at me, not making a sound, shock beginning to take over.

I strolled into the main room. "I got you a gift, Frank."

"What's going on? Why is my wife here?"

I walked around them, scratching my chin with the gun. "Imagine my shock when the crew discovered a new child pornography ring and Carly's name came up as being part of it."

"Impossible," he sputtered.

I stopped in front of them, ignoring his denial. "Then, when we dug further, we discovered she had help—*your* help."

He shook his head. "*Lies*, Matteo. All lies. You know I'm loyal. I would never…"

I narrowed my eyes, pointing my gun. "Filth, scum—the lowest of humanity that preys on the weak and the defenseless. The very basis of what we fight against, and now I find out you're one of them?"

"No, no…"

I cocked my head to the side. The rest of my crew leaned against the walls, watching. I could feel their hate growing. Frank had never fit in. He was never part of us. Julian had been blind to his weakness. When I presented the evidence to him of Frank's activities, he had been horrified, then only nodded as he closed the file. His silence effectively gave me permission for what I was going to do.

I pointed the gun between them, cocking the hammer. "I have proof that one of you is part of this. One of you speak up. I'll spare the other."

Carly pushed to her feet. "It was Frank! It was his idea —he said with all the contacts you had, he could find everything he needed to make his own ring! He wanted to make millions, and he didn't care who he hurt!"

I had planned to set them up, pitting them against each other, playing Russian roulette with the gun. I wanted to watch them throw each other under the bus and fight for their lives. But Evelyn had changed that plan. I no longer knew where the empty chambers were.

I squeezed the trigger, the pleading look on Carly's face turning to shock. She sank to the floor, grasping her chest as blood spread, pooling around her.

Frank stared at her, no emotion showing on his face. He turned his head, a sneer on his face. "I knew she was up to something. And trying to pin it on me. You can't trust a fucking woman. Right, Boss?"

I spun the chamber and lifted the gun. "You can't trust anyone."

He was dead before he hit the floor.

There was an odd sound from the room behind me. I glanced over my shoulder. Evelyn was hunched over, dry heaving. She rested her head in her hands, her shoulders bowed in pain and despair. She was tiny in the chair, all alone in the dark room, waiting to die. Even worse, *wanting* to die.

I glanced down at the bodies at my feet. I should feel shame. Guilt at taking human life. All I felt while looking at them was disgust.

"Marcus."

He approached. "Yeah, Boss?"

"Get rid of them. Liquidate everything they had. It all goes to the fund."

"I'll get Alex to start right away."

"Yes."

"What about her?" He indicated Evelyn with a lift of his shoulder.

"I need a wet cloth. A bottle of water."

"Um, Boss?"

"And bring around the car."

He opened his mouth to speak then, seeing the look on my face, changed his mind.

"Okay."

I held out the gun. "You know what to do." I nudged Frank's foot. "I want his memory wiped away. Completely. His name gets no respect."

"I'll make sure of it."

"Good."

I waited patiently until Marcus returned, bringing with him the items I asked for. I felt nothing as I stared at the two dead bodies except grateful that they could no longer hurt anyone. Teams were already breaking up the ring they had started—punishing the instigators and helping the victims. Many other bodies were hitting the ground tonight. They could all burn in hell.

Marcus handed me the cloth and water. "We'll finish here."

I nodded and walked around him, headed for the office and the woman.

I approached Evelyn, my hands held out. She was a huddled mass in the chair, shaking like a leaf. She lifted her head, meeting my eyes, certain of her fate.

"I'm not going to hurt you."

Her mouth opened and closed. No sound came out.

I handed her the cloth. She stared at it, making no move to use it. With a low sigh, I tilted up her face, wiping it, then her hands. Her skin was pale and her hands cold. She was definitely in shock. I tossed aside the cloth.

I set the bottle of water on the desk. "I thought you might need that."

She attempted to reach for the bottle, but her hand shook so hard it fell over. When she finally picked it up, she couldn't control herself enough to open the cap. The bottle fell to the floor, rolling away, unopened. She stared at it, not moving.

I kneeled and picked up the bottle, wiping it on my sleeve. I twisted off the top and held it to her mouth.

"Drink."

She didn't move. Her eyes fixed behind me, her gaze vacant.

Maybe I had misjudged her. Perhaps this was too much for her and I needed to rethink my plan.

I grasped the back of her neck, pressing the bottle to her mouth. "I said drink."

She swallowed. Then again. She drank until the bottle was empty.

"Better?"

"Y—yes," she rasped.

"What did you just see?"

"You killed those people."

"And you're scared of me?"

She was honest. "Yes."

I stood. "Do you have any family?"

She bit her lip, lifting a trembling hand, pushing her hair off her face. A dark bruise skated the length of her cheek. My fists tightened at the sight of it.

"No. Not anymore."

"No friends to miss you?"

"No."

When they started cleaning up the bodies, her gaze shifted, and I snapped my fingers.

"Here. Me. Focus on me. Nothing else."

Her eyes flew back to mine.

"When I'm in the room, that's all you pay attention to. Nothing else, do you understand?"

"Okay," she whispered.

"You saw nothing. Do you understand me? All that—" I indicated the room behind me "—was nothing but a nightmare. Nothing happened."

"Nothing happened," she repeated.

I kept questioning her. Asking about her life. Any ties she might have. What she had done for a living. How she got to Toronto from Alberta. The last name of her lousy boyfriend. Her replies were short and noncommittal.

Then I switched subjects.

"Where were you all night?"

"Walking."

"What did you see?"

"Nothing."

"Who did you talk to?"

"No one."

"How many people did you see get killed?"

It was the first time she hesitated. Then she swallowed.

"None."

I repeated myself, and she never faltered. Her gaze never strayed from my face. My determination grew, the inkling of an earlier idea solidifying.

"I have a problem, Evelyn."

"Me."

"Yes. No matter what you say, you did see something. You saw a lot."

"I know."

"I can't let you go."

A shudder ran through her. "May I please ask you something?"

I withheld my smirk. She was a fast learner. "Yes."

"Just kill me. Don't let anyone…"

I leaned closer. "Why are you so willing to die?"

"I have nothing left. Even if you let me go, Blaine will find me and either beat me to death or worse."

"Worse?"

She only nodded. Without explanation, I knew what she meant.

I was shocked when she reached out her hand, touching mine. Her skin was ice-cold, and I could feel the tremors racing through her. Strangely, though, I didn't mind her touch. I wanted to take her hand in mine and warm it.

"Please make it fast and give the money away. Don't let anyone else near me." A tear ran down her face. "Please, Boss."

Something flexed inside my chest. Something odd and unexpected. A need I had only ever felt for my family and the people I worked to save hit me in the chest. Evelyn, this small, frightened woman, had become one of those people.

I covered her hand with mine, the skin of her palm even colder. I chafed it gently.

"I can't do that, Evelyn."

She began to shake her head, getting ready to beg. I interrupted her.

"I can't kill you. I don't kill innocents." I allowed a smile. "I realize, considering what you saw, you don't believe me, but it's true."

"I—I don't understand. You can't let me go."

She was right. I couldn't let her go. I could hand her over to Julian, who would find her a safe place where she could start fresh. That would be the smart, logical thing to do. But it wasn't what I wanted to do.

I stood. "No, I can't." I raised my voice. "Vince!"

He appeared at the door, his massive shoulders almost filling the space.

"Is the car here?"

"Yeah."

"We're going to the house."

"Roger that."

"Call Geo and Father John. I want them both to meet us there. We'll be leaving in five minutes."

He hid his surprise. "Done." He turned and walked away.

Evelyn stared at me.

"I don't understand what's happening."

"Geo is my personal physician. He will examine you, so I know you're all right."

"And your father?"

I smirked. "Not my father. My priest."

Her brow furrowed. "You're going to make sure I'm all right, then he'll give me last rites?"

I shook my head, words I never thought I would say coming from my mouth. "No. He is going to marry us."

CHAPTER FOUR

Evelyn

After he made his announcement, I gaped up at the man standing in front of me.

"What?" I sputtered.

"I can't let you go. I can't kill you, so I have no other choice."

I looked over his shoulder to the room behind him, remembering what I had witnessed.

"You killed *those* people—I saw you do it."

He lifted one shoulder. "Yes."

"I expected you to kill me."

"We don't kill innocents. Ever. But I need your silence."

I pointed behind him. "They—they weren't innocents?"

"No," he snapped.

"I don't understand."

"I will explain it when I am ready. Not before."

I didn't know what to think. "But marriage…?" It seemed far too big a jump to comprehend.

He shrugged. "Insurance, if you will."

I frowned in confusion, my aching head making my thought process slow.

"Under the law, you can't be forced to testify against your husband. I already know you're a loyal person. You'll marry me for the protection I offer you. I will marry you for your silence, and…" He trailed off. "You'll be safe," he repeated.

"But those people…"

He pulled me to my feet, holding on to my arms when I swayed. "I already said I would explain when I'm ready to explain. You don't question what I do. How I do it. You need to accept this. Accept me." He shook me gently. "There's no choice here."

His voice was low, and he met my eyes steadily, no emotion showing.

He was right. What choice did I have? If he set me free, I would probably die. I was too weak physically to go too far, and Blaine would find me. But marriage?

"Will you hurt me?" I whispered.

His face softened, but he stood tall, and his voice was filled with conviction. "No. I will protect what is mine. I live in a violent world, but violence will never touch you. I won't allow it."

The dull light in the room emphasized the dark color of his eyes. As he studied my face, those eyes became liquid and warm. His expression changed, the stress leaving his face. He looked handsome, almost approachable. He raised one eyebrow quizzically. "Well?"

As if I had a choice in the matter. I had nowhere to go, no one to turn to. And for some reason, I found myself believing his words.

"No. I will protect what is mine."

"I don't know your name," I whispered.

He smiled; it was slight, but it changed his features. He stepped back, shrugging off his coat, draping it around my shoulders. "My name is Matteo. Matteo Campari."

"Why?" I breathed. "Why don't you just kill me? You don't know me. I don't mean anything to you."

He tilted his head, studying me. "I can't kill someone so beautiful and innocent, and whose only mistake was stumbling into a place she shouldn't. You've already been punished." He ran his finger down my cheek. "And you're wrong. You do mean something. Time will tell us what that is."

I shook my head, still confused. "But…why?"

He held out his hand, his tone brooking no argument. "Because I can." He waited as I stared at his outstretched palm. "Your choice, Evelyn. I suggest you choose wisely."

I let him lead me out of the building.

The car raced down the highway, the rhythmic sounds of the tires almost soothing. Beside me, like a silent sentinel, was Matteo. He had been busy on his phone, spitting out orders in the same foreign language he used earlier, and now he stared out the window.

"Were you...were you speaking Italian?" I asked bravely. I had recognized a few words, mostly curses, but a couple of the other ones were familiar as well.

"Yes."

"Ah. We're—we're going to your home?"

He studied me, then crossed his legs, running his fingers down the sharp crease of his pant leg.

"Yes. It is north of the city, in a private area. It will be your home as well. I think you'll find it comfortable."

"Will I—" I swallowed. "Will I be a prisoner?"

"No," he replied swiftly. "You will be protected. Cared for. Given the respect due as my wife."

My head ached with the turmoil and confusion of the past hours. I had been beaten, run terrified for my life, witnessed multiple murders, and now I was traveling in a luxurious car and being told I would be married to the stranger sitting next to me. It was all overwhelming.

I rested my head in my hands, startled when I felt Matteo cupping my face, his long fingers tenderly caressing my skull.

"You are in pain."

"I'm scared."

He lifted my chin, staring into my watery eyes. "I know," he said softly. "You are being very brave, Evelyn. You have a lot of inner strength." He smiled, wiping the tears on my cheeks. "You will need it over the next while."

"My dad—my dad called me Evie, not Evelyn. He said it was too big a name for someone so small."

A ghost of a smile played on his mouth. "Evie," he repeated. "Your father was correct. It suits you. Is that what your friends called you?"

"No, just him. You—you can call me that if you want," I offered, with no idea why I was doing so.

He nodded. "I will."

I swallowed my nerves, fingering the sleeve of his coat. The fabric was soft under my fingers, and the feeling soothed me. "What is going to happen now?"

His gaze took in my nervous handling of his coat. He shook his head, prying my fingers from the material. "Nothing bad. You'll settle into your new life, and I'll help you. You will find you are not alone in this."

"If I can't?" I dared to ask.

His dark eyes looked almost sad as he mulled over my question. "Then we will decide the next step."

"I'm so confused. My head aches and I hurt everywhere." A sob escaped my mouth. "I'm getting your coat dirty."

The last sentence came out of nowhere, ending on a high whimper. He looked startled then frowned.

"Do you expect to be punished for that?"

"Yes."

"It will not happen. You will never be struck again. I swear it." He tucked a piece of hair behind my ear. "I don't care about my coat. I'll have it cleaned or get another. I care that you are warm and dry."

"Why?"

He only smiled.

Then the car slowed, and he glanced out the window. The tint was so dark I couldn't see anything but dim lights.

"We're almost there. When we arrive, you don't ask questions. You don't fight. I expect you to show respect and act like a lady. Do you understand?"

A tremor ran through my body. "Yes."

I was surprised when his large hand covered mine. "I won't leave you alone, unless needed. I will help you through the evening. I know you're hurt and exhausted. I promise you, Evie, you will *not* be mistreated. You will never be mistreated under my protection. By me or anyone else. But I need your promise you will do as I ask."

His eyes were serious, his touch gentle, and his voice low. In that moment, he was only a man reassuring me. Despite what I had witnessed and what I knew he was capable of, my fear lessened at his promise. Hearing him call me Evie somehow helped to relax me.

"I will."

He squeezed my hand. "Good girl."

Those two words brought me inexplicable comfort. The odd sensation of wanting to please him surprised me.

I should be terrified. I had no idea where we were or what was going to happen next. I had only his word— that of a stranger—and yet, my fear had diminished since we left the warehouse.

Why, I had no idea.

When the car stopped, Matteo helped me out and escorted me up the steps. The house was large and grand, and I felt overwhelmed again. I looked around at the darkness behind me, nothing familiar, no streetlights to illuminate the area.

"You cannot run, Evie."

"I wasn't planning to," I replied, shocked to realize the words were true.

"Good. Come with me." Matteo headed up the stairs, and I followed, gasping when I stumbled. Matteo's arm shot out, steadying me. He didn't stop, sweeping me up into his embrace and climbing the steps. I felt astonishingly safe in his arms. The rational side of my brain reminded me I had watched him murder people, yet I felt no anxiety being close to him.

Did I really believe his promises?

Could I trust this man, or had my mind already decided he was the lesser of two evils? I had heard of Stockholm syndrome—was that what this was?

Inside, he climbed another huge staircase to the second floor. He set me on my feet in a spacious bedroom, sliding his coat off my shoulders. Then he urged me toward a door.

"The bathroom is there. Have a shower and clean up. I will return with Geo."

"My clothes..."

"My robe is on the back of the door. Clothes will come soon."

"O—okay," I whispered.

"You can do this, Evie. I have faith in you."

I could only nod. I had no choice.

The bathroom was large and opulent, with a step-in marble tub and a massive, double-headed shower. The floor was warm under my feet and the towels thick and luxurious when I touched them. I caught sight of myself in the mirror and grimaced. I had a large bruise on one side of my face, and my light-brown hair was matted with blood from where I had hit my head. My face was pale, my blue eyes standing out against my ashen skin. I looked drawn and terrified. There was no other way to describe it. I undressed, not surprised to see other bruises forming on my skin from Blaine's rough treatment. A few faded bruises were still showing from other times he had hit me. It felt surreal to think that the man whom I had watched murder people had touched me with greater care than the man who had professed to love me ever did. Even earlier in our relationship, Blaine's hold had always been too tight, and he often left marks during sex.

I shuddered, thinking about that. I had never enjoyed sex with Blaine. It had been rough and unfeeling and not satisfying most of the time. Especially after my dad died and Blaine had me completely in his grip. I glanced at the door to Matteo's bedroom.

Would he want to have sex as well?

Unable to think in that direction, I walked into the shower. It took me a few minutes to figure out how to turn it on, but once I did, the steam and heat helped ease the ache in my muscles. I carefully washed my hair and used the soap in the holder. It was rich and masculine, the scent that Matteo carried on his skin, reminding me once again of the stranger waiting for me. I quickly finished and wrapped myself in one of the thick towels, somehow not surprised to find them heated, the same way the floor was. I dried off and found a fresh toothbrush in the medicine cabinet to clean my teeth. I found a comb in the top drawer, and I used it to smooth out my hair.

I emerged from the bathroom, clean and wrapped in Matteo's long navy robe. I had to roll up the sleeves, and I tucked some of the trailing material under the belt. He was at least a foot taller than I was, if not more, and he outweighed me by at least seventy pounds. I stopped as I walked into the room, seeing Matteo waiting. His very presence made the room seem smaller. He was talking with an older man, their voices hushed. When he saw me, they stopped speaking, and he held out his hand. I went to his side.

"Evie, this is Geo. My uncle."

Geo stepped forward, holding out his hand in greeting. His silver hair gleamed, and his dark eyes were kind, his voice gentle. "Evie."

"Hello."

Matteo brushed my wet hair away from my cheek. "She was attacked, Geo. Her head was struck. Please check her over for me."

"May I?" Geo asked, addressing me, not Matteo. "I won't hurt you."

"Yes."

"Then let's get started."

Under Matteo's watchful eye, Geo checked me over. He was gentle, although a few times I winced, and once when he was examining my head, I whimpered as his finger touched a sensitive spot. Matteo hurried to my side, holding my hand.

"Careful, Geo."

Geo shook his head. "I need to see how deep the laceration is. I am being careful."

"It's fine," I assured Matteo, meeting his dark gaze. "Really."

He frowned but remained silent and stayed by my side the rest of the time. He cursed when he saw the bruises on my arms. I clutched the robe to my midsection as Geo probed the painful spot on my back. Matteo's cursing became louder, but he unexpectedly wrapped his hand around mine and lifted it to his lips, holding it to his chest as Geo finished. Matteo drew the robe back over my shoulders.

"Go sit over there, Evie." He indicated the love seat by the fire. "I've had tea and toast brought in. I would like you to eat."

I curled up, the soft cushions warm and welcoming. I poured a cup of tea, adding sugar and milk, and picked up a piece of the toast from a covered plate. I wasn't hungry, but again, I did as he asked, remembering his warning from earlier.

I felt his watchful gaze as Geo spoke quietly to him. Matteo met my eyes, nodding at Geo's words. He shook Geo's hand and waited until he left before coming over and sinking into the huge chair beside me.

He poured himself a cup of tea and lifted it to his lips. He sipped in silence, then sat back.

"Geo says nothing is broken, but he is worried about how hard you hit your head. I will watch over you tonight. He is going to bring a prescription for some painkillers to help your headache. His wife is big into natural treatments—essential oils and that sort of thing. She will bring something to rub into the bruises to help heal them quicker and ease the aches."

"That is very kind."

"You will be family now. They will look out for you as well." He cast his gaze over me, frowning when he saw a bruise on my foot. Blaine had stomped on it earlier in his anger. He leaned forward, tracing the darkening skin with his long finger.

"I can see how often you were mistreated from the marks on your skin. That will not happen again."

I believed him. "You don't have to marry me, Matteo."

He cocked his head to the side. "What is it you suggest I do with you, then, Evie?" he asked in a voice that was almost teasing in its tone.

"This looks like a big house. I could clean here. Or do the laundry. I'm a good cook. I could work for you, and you can keep an eye on me." I met his gaze. "I won't ever tell a soul about what I saw. I swear that to you."

He leaned forward, shifting on the chair so our knees touched. He stroked a finger down my cheek. "I know you won't. But I don't want you for a maid. I want you for my wife."

"I don't understand."

He sat back. "Frankly, neither do I. But somehow, I know this. I always trust my instincts. They have never failed me."

"Ever?"

"Not once. So, in a short while, we will be married."

"A license?"

He waved his hand. "All will be handled. You don't have to worry."

He stood, looking down at me. "You never have to worry about anything again, Evie. I'll take care of you. I promise your life is going to get better." He held out his hand. "And that is the end of the conversation."

CHAPTER FIVE

Evie

My mind reeled. A short time later, I stood in front of a stranger, a man I had witnessed murder four people, and married him.

Father John was a small man with a gleaming bald head. He looked pleased and didn't even blink at marrying us. Instead, he beamed as he pronounced us husband and wife. Matteo stood tall and handsome, wearing a deep-gray suit, the expression on his face somber. I wore a dark-blue dress Geo's wife, Lila, had brought to me. It was simple, with long sleeves which covered my bruises. My hair was down and my feet bare. I had no shoes. The old ones I had been wearing were filthy and unwearable.

She had introduced herself to me when she arrived, carrying the dress.

"I am Geo's wife." She smiled, laying down the dress on the bed. *Then she pulled out a small container. "I understand you are in*

pain, dear. If you would allow me, I can help ease the aches. This is essential oil cream I make myself."

At my wary look, she nodded in understanding, showing me a burn on her hand. "I did this only yesterday. See how well it already is healing. Geo swears by my elixir, as he calls it." She let me look at her hand then she offered to let me sniff the cream. It smelled lovely, eucalyptus, mint, and lavender hitting my senses along with other fragrances I couldn't identify.

She tsked as she saw my bruises and was gentle as she rubbed the cream into places I couldn't reach. Then she helped me dress, and I waited until Matteo reappeared to go downstairs. She had been very kind, which helped dispel some of my nerves—but not all of them. I was still overwhelmed.

I was shocked when Matteo slid a slender band onto my finger, then slipped his hand under my chin, lifted my face to his, and kissed me. His lips were soft and full, and his touch surprisingly tender. When he smiled at me, his eyes were warm, and he drew one long finger down my cheek.

"Forever," he murmured. "You are now mine forever."

I had no words to respond.

His men stood along the wall, witnessing our union. I signed the papers put in front of me, silent.

I sipped from the glass I was handed. As he promised, Matteo rarely left my side, his hand spread wide on the small of my back.

There were three other women in the room, aside from me—Lila, Gianna, and Roza, all of whom seemed friendly enough, although Gianna kept her distance. I knew she was Matteo's sister and was very uncomfortable around new people. I could understand her reticence right now, and I didn't approach her. In fact, I didn't approach anyone but remained where I was. Lila checked on me often, telling Matteo I should sit. He led me to a chair, gently pushing me down onto the cushion. He leaned down. "Are you all right?"

"Yes."

"This will be over soon." He frowned when I shivered, tucking my bare feet under the hem of the dress. "I will get something for your feet."

He turned and left the room.

Lila sat across from me, patting my hand in a maternal way. "You are very pale. Geo wants you to rest. I am sure the events today have depleted your strength."

I looked at her, unsure how to reply. I didn't know if I should talk, remain quiet, or give in and cry. I was lost.

She squeezed my hand. "I know you're scared. I know this must seem like a dream." She smiled kindly. "Or a nightmare."

I glanced down at my lap.

"Sometimes," she continued, "things are not as they seem. Matteo is a good man. Honorable. And despite what you may have witnessed, compassionate. Give him a chance. You may be surprised at what you discover."

"You—you know him well?"

"Yes, I have known him for a long time. He married you today and spoke sacred vows. I promise you—he takes his vows very seriously. He will take care of you." She cocked her head to the side, studying me. "I think you may be good for him."

Matteo reentered the room, carrying some socks. He kneeled in front of me, pulling the wool onto my feet, rolling it over on my ankles. They were too big and bulky, but the thickness felt good on my toes. "These will keep you warm." He reached up and stroked my cheek again. "You are doing well, Evie. Soon, you can rest, and tomorrow, we'll begin. All right?"

I glanced at Lila, who was watching Matteo fondly. I thought of what she had said. I heard the unexpected gentleness in his voice. His men were staring at him and the way he kneeled at my feet. They all looked shocked at his deferential position. I drew in a deep breath and smiled at him.

"Yes. Thank you, Matteo."

He stood and kissed my forehead. "Good girl."

As he moved away, Roza approached me. Tall and slender, she was elegant and pretty, with long dark hair and hazel eyes. "I'm pleased to meet you," she said, sounding as if sudden marriages at ten o'clock at night were a normal thing. "I look forward to getting to know you."

I smiled, unsure how to respond.

"I'm Alex's wife. He works for Matteo. And I work with the foundation here, so you will see me a lot."

"All right," I replied, unsure what the foundation was but knowing I would be told at another time. I was too exhausted to ask too many questions.

Like Lila, Roza seemed kind. She sat down next to Lila and leaned forward. "You will settle in here well, I'm certain."

I dared to ask. "How can you be so certain?"

"Because if Matteo thinks so, I trust him." She smiled. "He already holds you in high regard, or he would not have married you."

I wondered if she knew what had transpired tonight, then decided not to ask.

"Matteo has asked me to pick up a few things for you. Do you have a favorite color or style?"

"Um, blues and greens were always my preference." Blaine had gotten rid of all my clothes and dressed me all in black most of the time—uncomfortable, tight clothes I didn't like.

"Nothing overly tight or, ah…" I trailed off.

"Overtly sexual?" she guessed, studying me.

"Yes."

"With your coloring and size, I think soft and feminine —casual clothes would suit you best."

I relaxed a little. "Yes."

"I will bring you a few things tomorrow."

"I don't want to trouble you."

She and Lila laughed.

"Roza loves to shop," Lila offered. "She'll enjoy it."

"What size shoe?" Roza asked.

"Six."

"And about a four in clothes? A small, I think?"

"I prefer medium. I really hate tight things."

"Okay. I'll see what I can do."

"If it's not too much trouble, could I ask for a sweater? I, ah, have a lot of bruises on my arms, and they seem to upset Matteo. I would prefer to cover them up."

She nodded. "Of course. I will look after it."

"Thank you."

Not long after, Matteo clapped his hands, and the room dispersed. Lila and Roza each kissed me on the cheek, welcoming me to the family and assuring me they would see me in the morning. Gianna had disappeared already, leaving with the man I knew as Vince. Lila had told me he was her husband and very protective. That was all she said, but I saw the glimmer of sadness that lingered in her expression. It was yet another question in the long list of new things I would have to learn about this life and these people.

Matteo escorted me to his room, instructing me to wait for him. I sat, uncertain, looking around at the large room. It was expansive and extravagant, the king-sized bed prominent in the space. Heavy, masculine furniture and dark navy and rich cream made the room comfortable. The fireplace and furniture around it were inviting. I had seen the bathroom, and I assumed the other door led to a closet. I didn't investigate, though, still unsure of my place.

He entered, carrying a glass and a bottle of pills. He frowned seeing me sitting on the love seat. "You haven't changed or gotten ready for bed."

"I, ah…"

He shook his head. "Forgive me. I didn't think." He walked through the doorway to the room I hadn't looked in, coming out with a T-shirt in his hand, confirming it was a closet. He handed it to me. "This will have to do for tonight. Go and change."

"Am I sleeping here?" I asked bravely.

He tugged off his jacket, draping it over the chair. "You're my wife, so yes."

"I—"

"Relax. I expect nothing, Evie. Go and prepare yourself. I will wait here."

When I returned, he had changed as well, wearing a pair of sleep pants that hung low on his hips, and he was bare-chested. His torso and arms were well defined with taut muscles and his shoulders broad and strong-looking. There was a tattoo on his bicep, the black and red ink vivid on his olive skin. Without the veneer of his suit and with his hair mussed, he looked younger—more approachable. He held out his hand, and I took it, letting him lead me back to the love seat.

"Geo felt some mild painkillers would help you sleep." He showed me the bottle when I frowned. "They are not addictive, nor have they been altered in any way."

"All right."

Satisfied, he went into the bathroom, and I heard him brushing his teeth and the splash of water as he got ready to sleep. When he returned, he went back to the closet and came out with a bottle of cold water. "Geo is worried you may have a concussion. I'll check on you throughout the night."

"Why are you being so kind?"

"Is there a reason I shouldn't be?" His brow furrowed as he opened the bottle, shook out two pills into my hand, and handed me the water. I swallowed the pills, anxious for the relief they would give me. The Tylenol I'd had earlier had barely taken the edge off.

"Ah…"

"Don't mistake my kindness for weakness. I'm kind because you've given me no reason not to be." He stepped closer and cupped my cheek. "I hope you never do."

"I won't."

"Lila was talking to you."

"She told me you're an honorable man."

"And you think I'm a murderer."

I didn't deny it. But I had also seen something else in him tonight. Something human.

"I want to believe her. I want to get to know you."

He studied me for a moment, then tugged me from the chair and wrapped his arm around my waist, drawing me close. He laid his cheek on my head. "You smell like me."

I exhaled shakily, wondering why being so close to him didn't scare me. In fact, I liked it, which was even more confusing. I had stopped liking being touched by anyone.

But in his arms, I felt...safe, which was another odd reaction.

"I used your shampoo earlier."

He pressed his lips to my hair. "It smells good on you."

I lifted my head. He was so tall I had to lean back to see him. He smiled down at me, his dark eyes glittering in the dim light. "You are so beautiful, my wife."

I blinked at him. His tone was low, husky. Provocative. I couldn't recall the last time someone had called me beautiful. Thought me beautiful. Blaine certainly hadn't.

"What you saw tonight is only part of my life. I am more than what you think. If you give me the chance, I can prove it to you.

"I promise you, Evie, you will be safe. Protected. I will do everything in my power to care for you." He paused. "Be at my side, support me, and I promise, you will never have to fear anyone, including me."

I was mesmerized. His voice was a quiet, comforting murmur in the room. I found him compelling, and, strangely, I wanted to be close to him.

He traced a finger down my cheek. "I liked how it felt when I kissed you after our vows. Tell me, my wife, did you like it?"

"Yes."

He bent down, his mouth hovering over mine. "I'd like to kiss you again."

I felt myself tremble, shocked at the thought I wanted him to kiss me as well. His arms tightened, drawing me up his chest. His eyes drifted shut as his mouth slid over mine. Featherlight, tender, and warm.

"Touch me," he whispered.

I slid my hand up his arm, across his neck, and touched the hairs at the base of his head. He groaned low and covered my mouth again. He skimmed his tongue along my lips, slipping inside my mouth. I had never been kissed like that. Languidly, sensuously. His mouth moved over mine, harder, claiming me. He deepened the kiss, wrapping my hair in his hand and tugging my head to the side. Whimpers escaped my throat, desire beginning to build inside me. He lifted me easily, locking my legs around his waist, and holding me tight. I clutched his shoulders, lost in the sensations he created inside me. There was no doubt, no fear—only need. Need that he built and stoked. He broke from my mouth, dragging his lips down my neck. He pulled on my hair, exposing my neck as he licked and nipped. My head fell back, and I gasped in pain.

He stopped immediately, his eyes wary.

"I hurt you."

"No," I insisted. "My head…"

He cupped my neck. "I got carried away and forgot you're injured. Forgive me."

I blushed. "I–I liked it."

He dropped another kiss to my mouth. "So did I. And we'll explore this more when you're recovered. For now, I'm taking you to my bed, and I'll watch over you as you sleep. Tomorrow, we'll talk and figure out our new life together."

Why did that word bring me such pleasure?

Together.

What on earth was happening to me?

CHAPTER SIX

Matteo

The painkillers worked and Evie slept. I studied her features in the muted light. I had kept a lamp on in case she woke up and was confused. I didn't want to add to her already long list of anxieties.

She was beautiful. Her hair glimmered with subtle red in the light, and her long lashes rested on her cheeks, hiding her blue eyes I found bewitching. She was small but very feminine, with a full bust and curvy hips. I looked forward to the day she didn't cower and try to hide the marks on her body. I wanted to watch as she grew stronger and confident. I had a feeling she would be a force to be reckoned with.

The very second I had seen her in the deserted building, something stirred within me. A deep, protective feeling, an almost frantic need to ensure her safety, had overtaken me. Despite what she had endured, there was an air of innocence about her—a sweetness that lingered. I found myself wanting to be shown that sweetness. The first time I touched her, a strange sensation of something relaxing inside my chest caught me off guard. It was unsettling.

When she woke and saw me standing over her, the fear in her eyes was nothing new to me. Yet with her, I wanted to erase that fear.

I knew she had seen too much, and I needed her silence. However, I wasn't lying when I told her I didn't kill innocents. My job was to protect them. I could have arranged to send her somewhere far away and have her watched and looked after, but something told me this small, frightened woman was in dire need of protection that only I could provide.

When she tried to kill herself, I knew there was only one option. The idea to marry her came out of the blue, but once it entered my mind, its sheer simplicity and rightness took hold, and I could not shake it. Intuitively, I knew it was right. How? I had no idea, but I always trusted my instincts. She needed me, and on some level, I was certain I needed her as well.

She was willing to die, obviously not caring about returning to the life she led. As such, as an alternative, I could marry her. She could leave behind the life she knew and join me in this one.

I wasn't a benevolent man. I wasn't given to gentleness or affection. The world I lived in was cold, brutal, and filled with blood. Nonetheless, when I could remove myself for brief time periods, I liked the thought of spending them in her company. Kissing her earlier hadn't been in the plan, and her reaction to me was unexpected, but it pleased me. I had felt the roar of desire when my mouth was on hers, and with the way her body softened in my arms, I knew she felt it as well. I wanted to explore that with her.

My plan was simple. Tomorrow, Roza would help her with personal items, Alex would procure new papers, and I planned to punish the man who had so little regard for her well-being. It would be my wedding gift to her. I also had to pay a visit to my commander. I knew he would have heard I'd gotten married. Julian would be full of questions, and I would have to try to explain my actions and ask for his understanding. I was sure he would give it.

I couldn't explain my attraction to Evie to myself, never mind to Julian, but there was no denying it. The relief I had felt when she let me lead her from the warehouse had been undeniable. Her quiet dignity despite everything going on around her had impressed me. In spite of what she had witnessed, she had trusted me enough to take care of her, to fall asleep beside me in my bed.

I woke her again, making sure she was all right, then let her drift off once more. I ran a finger down her cheek as I made plans. I would take Evie away for a few days to my island. It was private, isolated, and perfect to get to know each other. I would tell her of my life and my expectations for her. She could heal, rest, and come to terms with her new life.

She shifted, rolling onto her back, a frown crossing her face before she relaxed again. The blanket twisted, exposing her bare shoulder. The shirt she wore was far too big on her, but I liked seeing her in it. Her creamy skin beckoned, and I thought of how she felt in my arms. How she tasted under my tongue. Her passionate response. Desire began to build, but the dark mark of fading bruises cooled my ardor. The rage I felt knowing she'd been abused was only matched by the anger I felt toward the men and women who took advantage of the helpless. For the first time in my life, the need to care for someone, to look after them, was prominent. I could understand Vince's unerring care for my sister a little better now.

Evie shifted again, rolling and curling into herself, a small whimper escaping her lips. I moved closer, carefully wrapping an arm around her. She settled against my chest with a small sigh, her warm breath blowing on my skin. I felt her sock-covered feet press on my legs, making me smile. I would have to make sure Roza got her some socks of her own. Maybe some of those fuzzy ones women seemed to like. Evie snuggled closer, almost burrowing herself into me. I felt a sense of satisfaction at her unconscious need to be close to me. Perhaps, deep down, she sensed the same draw I did. Her body certainly felt as if it already trusted me. Soon, I hoped her heart and head would follow. I would do everything I could to let her see the man I really was— not the one she thought me to be.

Then we would explore a physical relationship. I wanted her. I wanted to feel her under me, to bury myself inside her, and fill her with my seed.

We would be married in every sense.

She would truly be mine.

EVIE

The sun was bright when I opened my eyes in the morning. Matteo had woken me several times in the night, his low voice a murmur in my ear. He would ask me my name, his name, and how I felt. Once he was satisfied, he let me go back to sleep. He made me take sips of water, and at one point, when I told him my head was pounding, he gave me more painkillers. I was certain I had felt his arms around me, the heat of his body pressed to mine at different moments in the night, but when I woke up, I was alone.

There had been a tray with coffee, breakfast, and a note instructing me to stay in the room until Roza showed up. I had a shower, sipped some coffee, then waited, trying to sort through my feelings. My head still hurt, but not as badly. The cream Lila had given me helped ease the aches from the bruises. She had been kind enough to help me treat some of the bruises on my back I couldn't get to, and this morning, I felt the difference.

I glanced at my hand, looking at the pretty ring Matteo had put on my finger. The filigree and diamonds caught the light. Yesterday, I was running for my life, and today, I was married to a stranger for whom I should feel nothing but revulsion, yet who instead brought out some sort of yearning in me I didn't understand. His touch didn't frighten me—in fact, I wanted more. His mouth on mine had caused a maelstrom of feelings to well inside me. What I should feel and what I did feel were at war with each other. I should be looking for a way to escape. Looking for a phone to call the police and beg for help. Demanding Matteo release me.

Instead, I sat in the chair he'd been in last night, his scent encircling me, making me wish he were here. I had no desire to leave the confines of this house, somehow knowing, with him in it, I was safe and protected. There was a part of me that hoped he would kiss me again.

It was all very confusing.

Roza knocked and entered with a flourish, her hands filled with bags, followed by her husband, Alex. She immediately had me change into a blue shirt and brushed my hair back off my face. She added a little makeup, and Alex took my picture. They were kind and patient, but I knew better than to question them. I did only as I was instructed.

After Alex left, Roza spread out her purchases, telling me to pick what I liked, and she would return the rest and get me anything else I wanted and needed.

I looked at the pile of clothing on the bed, unsure how to respond.

"What's wrong, Evie?"

"I thought you were getting me a few things," I confessed. "I–I don't think I have enough money for all these clothes." My wallet was in my jacket, which was gone, and I had given Matteo the cash I'd stolen from Blaine. The price tags on the items showed they were all expensive.

She laughed, patting my arm. "Matteo told me to buy them. I have his credit card. These are for you, so you don't have to walk around in his robe and shirt. Once you feel better, you can get more clothes and things." She shook her head. "Matteo will look after you."

"Oh." I picked up a bathing suit. "I'm not sure I'll need this."

"Oh yes. There is an indoor pool here that is lovely, as well as an outdoor one. And Matteo says you'll need some light clothes for your trip."

"My trip?"

She bit her lip. "I think he is taking you away for a few days. Like a honeymoon."

I dropped my gaze, shocked. A honeymoon? Somewhere alone with Matteo?

I thought of his drugging kisses from the previous night. The way I felt pressed to his hard body. I had felt no fear or worry. Only a burning desire for more. More of him. It had shocked me. I knew I should be trying to figure out how to get away from him, but I didn't want to. His promises echoed in my head. Safety. Protection. *"I don't kill innocents."*

Despite what I had seen, the horror and blood, the only thing Matteo had shown me was patience. He was stern and demanding, but he hadn't been unkind to me. In fact, he had shown me more care in the short hours since the warehouse than Blaine had shown me our entire relationship.

Matteo asked for only one thing. Loyalty.

I could give him that.

Then I glanced at the bed and saw the flutter of lace and the gossamer lingerie in the piles. My breath caught.

He was going to ask for something else.

I thought of his mouth moving with mine. The heat of his body and how it felt when he touched me.

Could I give him that?

I looked at Roza, who was watching me, a smile playing on her lips.

I decided that maybe I could.

I ventured downstairs, dressed in the soft yoga pants, a pretty shirt, and a light sweater Roza had picked out, all in shades of green and gray. My feet were encased in sneakers and warm socks that didn't hurt my bruised flesh. I brushed my hair off my face, leaving the bangs to cover the discolored skin. Unlike the clothes I'd been forced to wear by Blaine, in these, I felt warm, safe, and covered.

I found the kitchen, stopping as I entered. Matteo was leaning on the counter, listening to an older woman with gray hair as she spoke. He held a cup of coffee in one hand, bracing himself against the counter with the other. He was focused on whatever she was saying, and it gave me a moment to observe him. His commanding presence was evident, his shoulders set back even with his casual pose. His hair was once again slicked back, his eyebrows dark slashes that emphasized the male beauty of his face. He held a mug in his long fingers, and I recalled how gently they had touched me. Not wanting to interrupt, I lifted my hand and rapped on the doorframe.

He glanced my way, the expression on his face softening. "Ah, here she is." He set down his mug, crooking his fingers. "Come in, Evie. No need to knock," he said, gentle amusement lacing his voice.

I crossed the room, and he took my hand, raising it to his lips. "How pretty you look today," he said. "Very fetching. Wouldn't you agree, Mrs. Armstrong?"

"Indeed, she is lovely."

Matteo introduced us, and she shook my hand. "There is coffee if you like."

"Thank you."

"Breakfast?"

"Oh, um, no thank you."

She frowned but didn't push. "I'll make you a good lunch. You'll have to tell me your preferences. And when you're ready, we can go over the household and what you want changed, Mrs. Campari. I'm going to go and check on the yard workers. They missed some weeds last week." She shook her head. "Lazy scamps."

She left, and Matteo drew me into his arms. It felt right to be nestled into his chest, his scent—cedar and fresh-cut grass—surrounding me. I felt the press of his lips on my forehead. "You are still pale, my wife. I want you to rest. And please eat."

"I will."

He drew back. "I'm sure you have questions. I promise to answer them when I can. I have a very busy day and I have to be gone for a while, but I'll be here later."

I stiffened in sudden anxiety. "You—you're leaving?"

He smiled in understanding. "I am leaving Marcus with you. He is my most dependable right-hand. He will guard you. There is no one I trust more to look after you."

"What about you? Don't you need looking after as well?"

His eyes softened, the flecks of gold around his pupils mesmerizing. "Vince will be with me." He stroked my cheek. "I like that you are worrying about me already." He shook his head. "I meant what I said last night, Evie. You are safe here. No one will find you, and you will come to no harm under my protection. Even if I am absent, you are protected."

"Should I stay in my, ah, our room?"

"No, this is your home. The only place off-limits is the office I work in. It's on the other side of the house. I ask you don't go in without me there and that you knock before coming in." He paused, meeting my eyes. "What I do—" He stopped and shook his head. "Promise me, Evie."

"I promise."

"Roza or Lila will show you around if you want. Marcus will not be far. There is a large yard and a garden if you enjoy that. Do not leave the gates. They are locked for a reason. If you leave the grounds, it will be with me or Marcus beside you. At least for now. Do you understand?"

"Yes."

He bent and brushed his lips to mine. "Thank you. I will see you this evening. Anything you want, anything you need, ask Mrs. Armstrong or Marcus. Or Roza if you are more comfortable."

"Can you finish your coffee before you go?"

His smile was wide. "Yes, I can."

I wandered through the large house, sticking to the main floor for now. Marcus was a silent sentinel behind me. He greeted me with a simple tilt of his head and a "Mrs. Campari" when I left the kitchen. Aside from his murmuring into his wrist on occasion, we engaged in little conversation.

A large central entryway divided the house into two sections. I quickly surmised one side was lived in and the other for business. I avoided the hallway I could see leading to that side of the house. I recognized a few of the men from last night, and I felt a case of nerves seeing them again. Marcus strode down the hall and shut a large doorway, effectively closing off the sight and sounds coming from the many offices and rooms I glimpsed. There was another office which I assumed was Matteo's, but for the moment, I didn't ask. He would show it to me when he was ready.

I discovered a large library, the shelves filled with books. I ran my fingers over the spines, imagining myself curled up in one of the tall wingbacks by the stone fireplace on a cool day, enjoying the warmth and losing myself in the words. Like Matteo's bedroom, it was a masculine room, the furniture heavy, the colors subdued. Still, I liked the feel of it.

Aside from the room we'd been married in the night before, a smaller, cozier room was located at the back of the house, with a TV mounted on the wall and a deep, comfy-looking sofa. The dining room was a long, formal room.

The pool was at the back of the house, glassed-in and inviting. I bent and ran my fingers through the warm water with a sigh. I loved swimming.

"Am I allowed to use this?" I asked.

"Of course," Marcus replied.

"With you watching me?"

"No. Inside the house, you are safe. If you go outside, though, I will accompany you. Mr. Campari thought you might have some questions as you looked around today that I could answer for you."

"Have you been with him long?"

"Yes."

"Do you—do you live here?"

"I have a place over the garage, yes. I stay there when required. I am close if you ever need me, Mrs. Campari."

"Do others live here?"

"Mrs. Armstrong has the other apartment over the garage. Vince and Gianna have a house set back on the grounds. You can see it from the great room."

"Ah."

I found an unused room with large windows showing off the massive, walled-in yard that ended at the tree line. I could see another pool, a tennis court, and a huge, covered area, obviously meant for entertaining. With a start, I realized my new husband was wealthier than I had already thought he was. It was disconcerting

I looked around the room—it was smaller than most of the others I'd looked at, and I wondered if Matteo would allow me to make it into a spot for myself. Somewhere I could read or do crafts. I used to love to sew and make things with my hands. I would build up the courage and ask him.

Another hallway at the back led to the other side of the house, and I glanced at Marcus.

"More offices. The ladies work there. You can go see them if you want."

My head was beginning to ache again, so I declined. "Maybe tomorrow."

I returned to the large room we'd been married in—the "great room," Marcus had told me. It suited the name. It held lots of seating with artfully arranged groupings, yet another fireplace, and high ceilings. It was the biggest room I had seen so far, and my least favorite.

At the end of the chamber were French doors that led to the outside. I paused with my hand on the handle. Marcus inclined his head, and I stepped outside, welcoming the fresh breeze. I walked the grounds, stopping to smell the flowers, look at the pool, admire the garden. I used to garden with my dad, and I enjoyed it. It might prove to be a good pastime here. Farther back, I saw the pretty house set in the trees where Vince and Gianna lived. I wondered if she would warm up to me.

I had a feeling I was going to have a lot of free time on my hands.

Finally, I went inside and returned to the kitchen. I told Marcus I was going to lie down after I ate, and he nodded, disappearing down the hall. Mrs. Armstrong presented me with a lovely salad, loaded with chicken and cheese, and sat talking to me while I ate. She told me Matteo was a pasta lover, preferred meat to chicken, occasionally ate fish because she made him, and had a sweet tooth.

"I love to bake cookies," I told her.

"I'll see the pantry has all the supplies," she assured me.

"Have you been here long?"

"Oh." She waved her hand. "Many years. I was with Mr. Campari before he moved here as well. Going on twelve years."

"That is a long time."

She nodded. "He works too hard. What he does——" She shook her head and clucked her tongue. "I'm glad he found you. I've been praying he'd find his own angel to help him. He needs his own life."

I wasn't sure how to respond. It was obvious she was fond of him and knew what he really did for a living. But I didn't question her.

She was pleased when I told her to carry on with her normal routine. I had no experience running a huge house like this and wasn't sure Matteo really wanted me to butt in. When she told me she had the weekends off as well as every second Monday, I assured her I would happily cook on those days. She beamed at me. "Good. I will not have to cook ahead for Mr. Campari, then. I usually go see my daughter and grandkids, and I always worry he won't eat, otherwise."

After lunch, I returned to our room, not surprised to find all the clothes and items Roza had purchased were put away. I peeked in the massive walk-in closet, feeling as if I was trespassing as I stepped in, looking at the contents. Matteo's suits, shirts, and pants hung in rows of military alignment along one side. There were pull-out drawers of T-shirts and other items, and a full-length mirror at one end. The other side held my new clothing, and I ran my hand over the items, smiling at the softness of all the fabric. Not a black piece of clothing in sight. Greens, blues, pinks, and other pastels filled the hangers. Pretty skirts and blouses were hung up, more soft yoga pants and casual clothing filled some of the drawers. Lacy lingerie occupied another. A new robe hung on a hook, the brilliant green silk soft under my touch. My half of the wardrobe looked empty still, yet I had never had so many clothes to choose from. The bathroom held a dizzying array of lotions, makeup, and other toiletries. I wandered back to the bedroom, sitting on one of the chairs, and looked around. Unbidden, tears sprang to my eyes, and I held my face in my hands and sobbed.

Strangely enough, they were tears of gratitude and relief and nothing else that I shed.

The next two days went by, equal in their passage of time. I swam in the pool, enjoying the unexpected luxury of having the whole pool to myself. I did laps, floated a little, and splashed around like a kid since there was no one to tell me to stop.

I saw Matteo only occasionally during the day. People came and went. I heard him talk, yell, curse, often in Italian. I caught glimpses of him pacing, entering his office or the other room, always shutting the door behind him. He issued orders, and they were never questioned. Long silences happened, and Lila confirmed they were studying information on a case. That was all she would tell me when she popped in for coffee, instead talking about the house or the weather.

However, when I did see him in person, he was patient and steady with me, never losing his temper. On the second day, while Mrs. Armstrong was out on an errand, I made him a sandwich, noting his usual lunchtime had come and gone. I had also noticed he yelled more when he was hungry and thought it might make things easier on his men if he ate now instead of waiting for Mrs. Armstrong to return. Unsure what he liked, I made him a sandwich the way my dad always liked it. Piled high with meat and cheese, fresh tomatoes, thinly sliced red pepper, and slathered with mayo.

I gave it to Marcus, asking him to deliver it to Matteo, and I sat down to eat a much smaller version of the sandwich at the table by the window.

I was surprised when the door opened and Matteo walked in, holding the plate and the untouched sandwich. I felt a flash of disappointment, which evaporated when he set down the plate and bent to kiss my mouth. "My wife made me lunch. How utterly… delightful," he murmured.

He sat beside me, quiet, lost in his thoughts as he ate. He wiped his mouth when he finished. "Delicious."

I smiled, pleased he'd enjoyed my simple offering.

He tilted his head. "You've been using the pool."

"I like to swim."

"Would you like some things for the pool? Toys, a lounger to float on when you're not doing laps?"

"You've been watching me?"

He smiled. "I peeked in. If I didn't have to meet with my men, I would have jumped in and splashed around with you."

My cheeks warmed in embarrassment. "I was enjoying it."

"Good. I'll have a few things brought over from the pool house."

"Thank you."

Nodding, he leaned forward, taking my hand. "You are feeling all right?"

"Better, yes."

"You've been crying."

"What?"

He traced under my eye. "When you cry, your eyes look gray. They reflect your emotions. Are you still frightened, Evie?"

I had cried again this morning while swimming. Every so often, a swell of relief hit me, mixing with the odd feeling of wellness. I hadn't felt safe and content in so long that, at times, I wasn't sure how to handle the thoughts. They seemed so foreign, given the man I was now married to and the life I was leading.

"No. I'm still finding my place, but I'm not frightened," I said truthfully. "Everyone has been kind. Sometimes, I just feel overcome, and the tears start."

He opened his mouth to say something, then closed it. He stood and bent, weaving his fingers through my hair and tilting up my head. "Your place is with me now." He pressed his mouth to mine. "I am happy you are here. More than I can express. Thank you for my lunch and the gift of your company." He strode from the kitchen, leaving me blinking after him.

I was beginning to crave his touch. He was never there when I went to bed, but I felt him in the night. He would slide in behind me, pulling me to his chest. As soon as he was there, I drifted into a deep sleep, feeling strangely safe in the arms of a man I knew to be a murderer.

Except I was beginning to think there was much more to him.

The next day, Marcus informed me Matteo wanted to see me in his office. I entered, looked around, curious and nervous. It was a large room, with lots of chairs and a couple of sofas. A long table was at one end of the office. Wide windows had a film on them, so the room was dimmer than the rest of the house. I knew all the windows were bulletproof. Marcus had told me that when I had noticed the different types of glass during our tour.

"Sit," Matteo instructed, not looking up from a pile of papers.

I sat, stomach churning. Had I done something? Gone somewhere I shouldn't? Outside, if I ventured too far, Marcus would make a low noise in his throat, and I would step back closer to him. The high fence seemed to cause him the most displeasure.

"Did I–did I do something, Matteo?" I murmured, my throat dry. "I didn't mean to."

He looked up with a frown. "Not at all, Evie." There was a knock at the door, and he looked behind me with a smile. "Ah, Mrs. Armstrong. Good timing."

She came in smiling and slid a tray onto his desk. "You enjoy," she said brightly and departed in her cheery, efficient manner.

Matteo indicated the tray. "I wanted to have lunch with you again. I thought we could eat in here, then talk a little."

"Oh."

He sat back, regarding me, his look indulgent. "What are you feeling guilty about, Evie? The rose you picked in the garden this morning? The splashing in the pool? The chocolate you snuck from the box last night? The croissant you didn't eat at breakfast?"

I stared at him. I was shocked when he winked at me.

"I'm a busy man, but I watch you."

"Why?"

"You mesmerize me."

I didn't know what to say.

He pushed a plate toward me. "It won't be as good as yours, but have your sandwich. You aren't eating enough, and I have plenty to worry about without adding your health to it."

"I'm not eating enough?" I repeated.

"No. Mrs. Armstrong tells me you barely pick at your food. I noticed yesterday you ate half of your sandwich. She told me you hardly touched your pasta last night." He met my gaze. "If I have to sit with you to make sure you eat, I will, *Piccolina.*"

I had no idea what piccolina meant, but the way it rolled off his tongue, it sounded affectionate.

So, I picked up my sandwich—because he asked me to.

What was happening to me?

One of his men walked in, a sheaf of papers in his hand. "Matteo—"

"Not now," he barked.

"But—"

"Leave," Matteo snapped.

I cringed at the sound of his voice, the tone reminding me of the night in the warehouse, but once the door shut behind me, he relaxed and asked me if I wanted more iced tea, his voice its usual patient tone.

I blinked at the sudden change in his demeanor, wondering if I would ever get used to his fast-shifting personality.

After we ate, Matteo rounded the desk and sat beside me. "We're leaving tomorrow."

I swallowed. "Where are we going?"

"I am taking you on our honeymoon."

"Oh."

He handed me an envelope. Inside was a new driver's license and passport, both with the name Evie Campari.

"The birthday is wrong."

He sat back, rubbing his finger over his chin. "No, it's not. You have a new name, a new birthday, a new life." He met my gaze. "Evelyn Gail Harper is dead. Evie Campari is the only name you have now. I thought you'd want to keep the name your father liked to use."

"I don't understand."

"Last night, Blaine Newson was arrested on murder charges. A woman matching your description and carrying your ID was found, beaten and strangled. His DNA was all over her."

I blinked and gasped.

"He's in custody." He grinned—a cold, frightening grin that reminded me exactly who he was. "He won't make it to the trial."

I began to shake as I processed Matteo's words. I knew I should feel bad for Blaine. But the only thing I felt was relief.

"The woman?"

He shook his head. "A Jane Doe. She was not harmed to help you. Don't ask."

I nodded with a long exhale.

"You have no family, and as you told me, you know nobody here and few people to miss you where you came from. Your old life is over. You are my wife, and you will be safe. He will pay for hurting what is mine." His fingers drummed on his knee. "For hurting an innocent."

"Is—is that what you do?" I asked. "Kill those you decide deserve it?"

"Do you really want to know?"

"Yes. I need to understand. Are you with the mafia?"

"All you need to know is that I work with an organization of considerable power. I run a very elite crew."

"You kill people. You're an assassin—a gun for hire."

He chuckled, leaning forward, running a finger down my cheek. "No, I'm not a gun for hire. You watch too much TV."

"I don't understand."

"Always so curious, *Cara*," he murmured, cocking his head to the side.

This time, I knew what that word meant, and I felt myself blush. He took my hand, spinning the ring he'd placed on my finger around as he spoke.

"I was just a normal kid. We lived in Little Italy, my dad was a cop, and my mom stayed home. We were ordinary. We weren't rich or affluent. But when I was fifteen, Gianna was kidnapped. My life changed overnight. Every waking hour was spent trying to help my dad find her. My mom was a lost cause, crying and drinking all the time."

I flipped my palm, interweaving our fingers. "What happened?"

He looked at our joined fingers and frowned. "My dad was one of the good guys, you know? He tried, but he had nothing. Just a bunch of dead ends. Even his fellow officers thought she'd just run away. There was no ransom note, nothing. They'd seen it too often and were sure she'd gone off on her own."

"But she hadn't?"

"No. I saw it happen. I saw the men who took her. No one believed me except my dad. Everyone said what I saw was my sister going out with friends. I knew it was something different." He rubbed his eyes. "One night, I snuck out of the house and went to a bar. My friend was always bragging about his uncle's illicit life and his ties to the underworld. The power he had. We went and found him. We told him what happened and what I saw. He believed me."

He inhaled. "Long story short, they found her. Brought her home. They even helped with counseling for her and my mother. And the day they did, in gratitude, I swore one day I would become one of them."

"What happened to your sister?" Gianna still hadn't spoken to me. I rarely saw her, and if I did, she averted her eyes.

"Gianna was messed up for a long time. She still is in many ways. But she got help, and she married her childhood sweetheart, who also happened to be my friend who got me to his uncle. You met him—Vince." He smiled. "She's protected—just like you are. He would die before he let anything happen to her. He is very good to her, and he understands her limitations. She loves him a great deal."

"And your parents?"

He grimaced. "They died in a car accident that was no accident."

I gasped. "What kind of accident?"

"Their car was run off the road on the way home one night. They'd gone to see Gianna at the facility where she was getting treatment. I was supposed to be with them, but I wasn't feeling well and stayed home." He was silent for a moment. "Vince's uncle came and got me. He was honest and told me the car was forced off the road and the evidence covered up. He was sure it was reprisal for getting Gianna back."

"Matteo," I whispered. "How awful."

He nodded, silent for a moment. "Aldo, Vince's uncle, took me in and cared for me, made sure I was safe. I became part of their family. When I was eighteen, they offered me a place in their organization."

"What about Geo?" I asked.

"He and my dad were estranged. As I got older, he reached out, and we became close. He knew of my decision and didn't try to change my mind. He joined me. He is a valuable part of my team."

"So, this organization offered you a place...?" I trailed off.

"Yes. It was what I wanted. It was a chance to help eliminate the world of people who prey on the weak and helpless. When Julian took over, he gave me my own team. We break up child pornography and slavery rings. We go after drug pushers, abusers, stalkers, kidnappers, and so many others."

"You're judge, jury, and executioner?"

"I'm part of the investigation team—and, yes, executioner. Once they're dead, we liquidate their assets, and all the monies go into a fund that supports the victims. If possible, we try to reunite them with their families, make sure they get counseling, help them back on their feet."

"Those people the other night…"

"They liked to get runaway kids hooked on drugs. Then they would sell them. And the man who was part of our team betrayed us. Betrayed *me*." His expression was furious, once again the avenging angel of death. "There is no gray in this area, Evie. It's black-and-white. He went against everything we stand for and chose money over innocent lives." He sat back, crossing his legs. "And he threatened you."

"Have you ever made a mistake?"

"No. Never. I have resources and people who make sure we target only the bad guys. The lowest of humanity. We rid the world of them."

"And you do it all from here? Right in the open?"

"My cover is in money markets—a highly successful business I run from my home. I am actually very good at it, but it is only a cover. A legitimate business to hide the real one. You won't find what I do listed anywhere or claimed by anyone, Evie. We are completely dark." He smirked. "The government knows of our existence, supports it even, but never acknowledges it."

I frowned in confusion.

"We save them a lot of time and expense. No wasting taxpayers' money on trials or taking up space in jails. We extract justice—immediately."

My head spun. Matteo stood, leaning against the desk. "That's the man you have married, Evie. It's not going to change. I'm not going to change. I know you're still confused. Worried. Unsure of your future." He paused, stroking his chin. "So, I'm giving you two choices. Consider them carefully because it will be the only time I make this offer."

His gaze was dark and serious. His shoulders tense. He looked like the Matteo I first saw, except I was sure I heard a trace of anxiety in his voice.

"And they are?"

"You can't leave. That isn't an option. You can stay here —and live a safe life. Read, work in the garden, cook, whatever you want. I'll set you up in an apartment on the grounds and ensure your complete safety."

"And what do you get out of it?"

"I get the satisfaction of knowing I saved another innocent from something terrible happening to them."

"What if you want to get married to someone else?"

"That isn't an option."

"What is my second choice?"

He kneeled in front of me. "You can join me in this fight—like Lila, Roza, and Gianna, helping the people we save. Making sure they're looked after. Whatever you want to do." He drew in a deep breath. "Get to know me, Evie. Be my wife in every meaning of the word—stand with me, support me. Maybe you can learn to love the man, not the job. We could have a family, if you want. I think if you gave yourself a chance, you could be happy with me."

"Is this something you will do for the rest of your life?"

"No. Everyone has their limit. This is my *for now*. But I have no plans of leaving it any time soon."

He took my hands. "Something happened the night I found you. I felt a protective instinct like nothing I had ever experienced. I couldn't bear the thought of anything happening to you." He shut his eyes. "When you grabbed that gun to kill yourself, I found myself praying for a miracle."

I shuddered, thinking of that night.

"The choice is yours. I won't force you into anything. If you think you can live with this reality, I promise you I will be a good husband to you." He leaned closer, pressing his warmth into me. "I felt something so strong when I kissed you, Evie. I want to kiss you every time I see you, if you'll let me. I thought you felt it too."

"I did."

His lips met mine and moved hungrily. With a groan, he yanked me close, deepening the kiss. I wound my arms around his neck, letting him explore, learning his taste and the feel of him. He drew back, leaning his forehead on mine.

"What do you say?"

There was only one choice to make.

"Take me on our honeymoon, Matteo. I want to get to know my husband. All of him."

CHAPTER SEVEN

Evie

Matteo was in a good mood. He had been since we'd landed on his island. Gone was the slicked-back dark hair and stern expression. Without gel, his hair fell over his forehead, giving him a rakish, sexy look. In the sunlight, the dark color showed bits of copper in his hair. His brown eyes danced with happiness, and he laughed. He had a loud laugh that boomed and echoed. It made me laugh with him.

We had spent the past two days exploring. Talking. Getting to know each other. He was well-read and intelligent. Without the restrictions of his team around him, he was relaxed and happy. He showed me all his favorite spots on the island, holding my hand, often kissing me. He was fascinated when I told him I had been a teacher. His eyes glowed when I told him how much I enjoyed teaching children, watching their faces as understanding dawned and they learned something new.

"You want children, Evie?" he asked, his voice pitched low.

"Someday," I responded, suddenly breathless.

The air crackled around us, then he stood and walked away.

At night in the darkness, he would snake his arm around me, holding me tightly, but that was all. I had expected him to advance our relationship. Instead, he had stalled it. I was confused, frustrated, and feeling off-kilter. I wasn't sure what to do or how to bring up the subject. He seemed impervious, nothing upsetting him. He swam, lay on the beach, soaked up the sun, and ate heartily.

He was sexy. The way he moved, the way he spoke. Most of the time, he was bare-chested, his skin turning more golden each day. His shorts or swimsuit hung off his hips, and he was casual and laid-back. I saw the way his eyes flickered when I would walk out of the house in a swimsuit or donned one of the pretty, short dresses I had packed, but he never reacted other than pushing his sunglasses up his nose and blowing out a long breath on occasion.

He was infinitely patient, showing me the coral reefs, guiding me around the caves, holding my hand when I was nervous. He was funny, telling me jokes and making me laugh. He loved to cook with me. He had a large wine cellar and made sure to pick a wonderful bottle every day, showing me how to taste it. He was everything a woman could want in a husband, except he didn't touch me.

But I craved him. I had never known desire for a man the way I did for Matteo. Heat pooled in my stomach when I would watch him through my sunglasses. Memories of his mouth on mine, how his body felt when he held me, would repeat in my head when he was close. The desire to reach out and touch him was something I fought every day. But I was too afraid to do so. Too nervous to speak up and ask him. I was ready for him—for everything. I had even had a birth control shot to make sure we were covered, and I had made sure he knew Geo had given it to me. My biggest fear was that he had decided he didn't desire me. Maybe once he'd seen me in the bathing suits Roza had picked up for me and discovered the lingering scars on my body, he'd realized I wasn't as attractive as he had thought.

On the third day, I woke up alone, my mood decidedly dark. I headed to the kitchen, knowing I would find Matteo there, cooking. He loved breakfast and enjoyed making it.

He greeted me with a warm smile, dropping a kiss to my mouth and handing me a cup of coffee.

"Good morning, my wife. The day promises to be another beautiful one."

I managed a smile, but I didn't say anything.

"I made pancakes." He set out a plate, piled high. His chest was bare, showing off his defined pecs and broad shoulders. His shorts hung low on his hips, his stomach taut, and that tantalizing V prominent. How was it possible for one man to be so sexy?

I had to look away. "Thank you."

He furrowed his brow. "Would you like some juice? I squeezed it myself."

"How domesticated of you," I said, sounding snarky even to my own ears. "No, thank you."

He sat down, silent, but filled his plate and began eating. I pushed mine around, my appetite nonexistent.

"Something wrong with the pancakes?" he asked.

"No."

He scowled, finishing his pancakes in silence.

I gave up pretending to eat and set down my fork.

"I thought a picnic on the beach today would be nice."

"Hmm," was my noncommittal reply.

"Or perhaps a clam bake later. We could dig some at low tide."

"I don't like clams."

"I can order some fresh lobster and shellfish to be delivered from the mainland, then. Grill them on an open fire on the beach."

"If you would like."

He pushed away his plate, pursing his lips.

"Would you like to try snorkeling today?"

I shrugged. "Whatever you want."

He crossed his arms. "My wife seems petulant this morning."

"*Really.*"

"I don't like it. Nor do I like your tone or the pouting mouth."

I knew I was acting like a child, but I didn't care. He made me angry, and I wanted to do the same. Deliberately, I pushed out my bottom lip farther.

"Do that again, and I'll bite it."

I rolled my eyes. "Well, that would be an improvement."

His eyes narrowed, and he spoke slowly. "Is there something you want, Evie?"

"Does it matter?"

"Yes. Tell me what you want." His voice dropped. "You might get it."

I slammed my hand on the table, my desire overtaking my fear. "You, Matteo! Dammit! *I want you*! I want you to make me yours—to make lo—"

He was on me before the last word left my mouth. Dishes flew off the table as he swept them aside, setting me on the solid wood surface.

"I thought you'd never break." He growled. "I thought I was going to die of blue balls on my honeymoon."

"I thought you didn't want me," I gasped.

He pushed my hand over his large erection. It pulsated under my touch. "Does this feel like I don't want you, Evie? I've been waiting for you to be ready."

He kissed me. Hard. Wet. Greedy. His tongue claimed my mouth, robbing me of any more words. He gripped the material of my robe, tearing it from my body, and his mouth descended, licking and sucking at my breasts.

"You are so fucking beautiful. You were made for me."

I cried his name when he cupped my pussy, his touch possessive. "This is mine now. *You* are mine."

"Yes!"

"I'm going to fuck you, Evie. Then I'm going to take you to our room and do it again. I'm going to make you come so often, you won't be able to stop. I'm going to fuck you until you can't remember anything but me. Your body won't ever want anyone else *but* me. Do you understand?"

I could only whimper.

He yanked off my underwear and stroked his fingers against me. "You're wet, baby. So wet for me." He slid one long finger inside, then a second. "So tight. *Jesus*, you're going to feel amazing wrapped around my cock."

I arched against him, lost to his dirty words and domineering touch. He was like a python, ready to strike, hovering over me, eyes hooded and dark. He played me like a violin, his fingers knowing exactly where to touch me, how to draw out my pleasure. His mouth covered mine as my first orgasm blossomed, taking over my entire body.

"My name, Evie. Scream *my name."*

It echoed in the room.

He ran his open mouth down my torso, teasing my stomach with his lips. He stood, tugging me up. I leaned against his chest, trying to catch my breath. A small part of me thought I should be afraid of his passion and dominance. But the rest of me ignored that little voice. Sex as I knew it before Matteo was nothing like this. It never would be again.

He lifted my chin, his lips at my ear. "I'm not done with you. Not by a long shot." He lowered his voice. "Look at me, my wife."

I opened my eyes, taking him in. He was naked, his skin golden and taut in the light. His cock was rigid, long, hard, and weeping for me. I leaned back, Matteo following me, his mouth demanding on mine. He surged forward, burying himself inside. I clasped his shoulders as he moved, my fingernails digging into his skin. The table creaked under his dominance, the legs scraping against the floor. He gripped the edge of the wood, pressing me into the hard surface. He slammed into me powerfully, never faltering as I exploded around him. I had never experienced sensations like this. Never felt orgasms so powerful I thought my body would tear apart at the intensity of the act. He rode it out, sweat dripping, our bodies sliding on the wood, then his head dropped to my neck, his body shuddering, and he finally stilled.

"Evie," he moaned, his breath hot on my skin.

I wrapped my arms around him, lost to everything he was. His heat, his strength, his lust. I would take it all for him.

He lifted his head, running his fingers over my mouth. "You're mine now."

"I already was, Matteo," I countered.

He gathered me in his arms and carried me to our room. With the curtains still drawn, the light was hazy and dim.

He laid me on the bed, his touch changing. It became light, gentle, indulgent. His mouth was warm and teasing on my skin. His words were low, adoring, and sank into my heart. They broke it open, and I accepted him the same way my body accepted his. We moved together as if we'd done it for a thousand years. The world narrowed down to just the two of us.

After, lying in his arms, I sighed.

"I thought you weren't gentle."

"You bring that out in me, *Piccolina*."

"What does that mean?" I asked.

He kissed my head. "Little one. It means little one."

He shifted to look into my eyes. "My tenderness—it is something you will only see in private. I need you to understand that, Evie."

"I do."

"What are you thinking?" he asked with another kiss to my mouth.

"That maybe I should be petulant more often...when we're alone, of course."

He chuckled. "Of course."

"Why did you wait?"

"I wanted to know you were certain. That you wanted me as much as I wanted you."

"I did. I do."

"Then, as of now, we are truly married. You are mine."

I snuggled to his chest. His. I liked that.

"I will never let you go, Evie."

Those words from anyone else would have frightened me. Coming from Matteo, they were a promise. A confirmation that I had a place in his life.

And God help me, I wanted that.

CHAPTER EIGHT

Matteo

E vie slept in my arms, the breeze blowing the curtains into the room. The skies outside were heavy with rain today, the wind kicking up the white on the ocean, the waves a mixture of gray and dark blue.

I couldn't recall the last time I was this relaxed. Content and happy. Every day with Evie was like another present I got to unwrap and discover.

She was clever and witty. Shy and sweet. Passionate and sexy when I lit the flame inside her. She had even instigated our lovemaking a few times, which delighted me to no end.

The first time she had dropped to her knees and taken me in her mouth was something I would never forget. The way her blue eyes stared up at me, her hair slicked off her face and the water from the shower clinging to her shoulders, running off her neck. She was hesitant, her confidence growing as she engulfed me, learning what I liked, what she liked. The heat of her mouth and the feel of her tongue were incredible, and I let my head fall back against the tile wall.

"Like that, Piccolina," I praised.

"Cara, mine. God, yes," I groaned when I felt her take me deeper.

I buried my hands in her hair, guiding her. "Suck me, Evie. Take all of me."

She scraped the underside of me gently with her teeth and suckled the crown. Then she sucked me deep into her mouth, and I lost it, coming hard, cursing, panting, growling out her name.

Afterward, I held her in my arms, frightened by her sudden weeping.

Had I hurt her somehow?

I rinsed her off and carried her to our bed, letting the breeze float over us as she calmed.

"Tell me," I demanded.

"Sex before——" She swallowed. "Sex before you was painful. Blaine held me down and forced himself on me at times. Oral sex was horrific. He used to, ah——"

Anger and rage built within me. "I will never force you."

She met my eyes. "I know, Matteo. You make me feel safe. You show me I'm safe. I have never considered that act anything but demeaning. But not with you. Everything with you is so incredible. I didn't mean to cry—it just hit me that you let me feel. You let me explore and try. And I want to try everything with you."

I cupped her face. "I look forward to it, my wife."

I tightened my arm around Evie, thinking of her passion. How, every day, she showed a little more of her true self to me. She became less afraid. More secure in the knowledge she was safe and would never be mistreated again.

Even now, I felt rage at the way she'd been abused. Blaine was dead—a fact I hadn't shared with Evie yet. He'd paid for his treatment of her, and before he died, he knew what he was being punished for. Part of me wished he were still alive so I could be the one who watched the realization dawn in his eyes as he departed this earth for hell. But I was glad he was gone and she would never have to fear him again.

My wife would never have to fear anyone as long as I was around. Nothing in my life would touch her. I was determined. I frowned as I recalled there were only a couple of days left of our honeymoon. All too soon, we would be returning to reality—back to the world I once inhabited without a thought. Now I had Evie, that had changed. For the first time ever, I didn't want to return to it. It was a strange feeling.

Evie awakened many strange feelings in me. Some I'd thought were long dead. The tenderness and care I felt for her deepened every day. The sense of rightness of having her by my side was certain and true. She was the softness I needed in my hard life. The sunshine to the constant dark that surrounded me.

She was becoming my focus.

She stirred, blinking awake and smiling at me.

"Good morning, *Piccolina*."

Her eyes were clear and bright blue. I loved them happy, the color showing her emotion so clearly. She'd lost that look of fragility, her body filling out, her confidence slowly emerging. Her hair had lightened in the sun, gleaming red and gold under the light. I'd arranged for a hairdresser before we'd left, and although they'd trimmed several inches off the bottom, it still hung past her shoulders. The hairdresser had added some highlights, which brightened the color and suited Evie. There was the faintest hint of tint on her skin from the sun. I made sure she was covered in block so she didn't burn. The freckles on her nose were a result of the days she forgot a hat, but I found them enticing and adorable. I loved to kiss them, tracing the faint glints of gold with my tongue.

"Hello," she whispered, her shyer side showing. I was never sure which woman I would wake up to—the passionate wanton who would straddle my hips, taking what she wanted, or the demure angel I had to coax to open up for me. Both were equally pleasing and sexy.

I nuzzled her lips, smiling as she ran her hand down my torso, featherlight and teasing. I groaned when she wrapped her hand around me, slowly stroking and running her thumb over the crown in a sensual drag that drove me mad with desire.

"What do you want this morning?" I murmured.

"Pancakes," she replied seriously.

I chuckled and rolled her under me. "You've woken the beast, my wife. He needs to be controlled first. Then you get your pancakes."

She wrapped her legs around me, cradling me with her body. I felt her desire as I slid through her heat. "If I must," she teased. "Your pancakes are so worth the extra effort."

I nipped at her lips. "I'll make it worth the work."

Her smile was bright, her eyes filled with so much emotion, I caught my breath. "I know, Matteo. I know."

Tenderness only she could inspire settled over me. I covered her mouth with mine, kissing her with long, languid strokes of my tongue. I caressed her, using my fingers to stroke her skin, my mouth to worship it, and my words to assure her.

"So beautiful," I murmured.

"All mine. Forever," I added when she sighed.

I groaned at the rightness of sliding into her. Feeling her clench around me. The passion in her gaze as our eyes locked. I slid my hands up her arms, locking them over her head as I moved inside her, the heat and clutch of her intense and perfect. I moved slowly, rolling my hips so we were never apart, our skin pressed together constantly. She moaned and whimpered, undulating with me, crying out in her completion. The sound of my name falling from her mouth did something to me. The part of me that was removed and broken knit back together, and I buried my face into her neck, breathing her name.

"Evie, I love you. I love you," I repeated as my orgasm crested.

When, how, the circumstances that brought us together, made no difference. She was my wife, my love, my world. I knew this with a certainty that shook me. She had become everything I wanted, everything I needed.

I lifted my head, meeting her teary gaze.

"I love you," I said again, wanting her to know how much. How real the feelings were for me.

"I love you too, Matteo."

Her words filled me with exultation. Her beautiful, expressive eyes showed me how true they were. She felt the same way I did. I was hers.

I crushed her to me. "I love you, Evie Campari. I will keep you safe. Always, my innocent, my *Piccolina*. You are safe with me. And I will love you always. I can't wait for you to join me in my life. I'm going to be even stronger with you by my side."

"I will never leave it."

I lowered my head and kissed her.

My perfect little treasure. My *tesoro*.

EVIE

I stared out the window as the plane began its descent into Toronto. The clouds opened up, and I looked at the city coming into view, trying to calm my nerves. The entire trip, Matteo and I had been silent. I heard him flipping through some files, tapping notes on his laptop keyboard, but the sounds had ceased a while back.

I couldn't bring myself to look at him.

To let him see my weakness and know he would already be disappointed in me.

The past weeks had been the best of my life. I'd discovered a very different side to my husband, and I was completely in love with it. With all of him, if I was being honest. His work was brutal and scary, but his reasons did, in fact, make sense to me. The bottom line was, if he hadn't been there that night, I would probably be dead. I would forever be grateful to whatever higher power brought us together.

I never expected to love Matteo. I knew I desired him, and the passion he brought out in me was new and exciting. But somehow, without realizing it was happening, I fell. Deeply, without limits or reservations. I saw the man behind the cold exterior. Felt the gentleness hidden by the rough gestures and impatient voice. I knew how great a gift that was. He allowed me to see the real Matteo. The human being capable of tenderness and warmth. It was a side few ever witnessed.

And he was mine.

Our days on the island were endless sunshine. We explored and laughed, made love in the ocean, on the sand, by the pool, in the pool, even in the dim caves we explored, our cries echoing off the stone walls. Matteo's desire was rampant, and all it took was a smile or crook of my finger, and it began. He was possessive and demanding, showing me what he wanted, what he needed from me, right at that moment. He, in turn, gave me pleasure I never knew existed. He was vocal, his movements sure and exact, coaxing orgasm after orgasm out of me, until I was spent and limp in his arms. The nights were spent in the huge bed, where he lavished me with kisses, claiming my body over and again, never seeming to get enough. His voice was gentle, his touch tender. His whispered words were filled with adoration. In the stillness of the dark was when I felt his love the most, when he felt free to be himself.

My husband. *My* Matteo.

I glanced down at my hand, the light catching the diamond band that resided there. Delicate and lovely, it nestled perfectly with the simple band he'd given me the night we married. He'd surprised me with it one morning, slipping it onto my finger while I slept.

"I didn't think you would like a large, showy diamond," he explained. "I had this made for you."

He was right. I loved the way the diamonds caught the light and how it sat on my finger. The stones were set in white gold, and the circle was endless, much like the way I felt for Matteo. No beginning and no end. It seemed so fitting, and I had felt so sure of my place with him.

But now, we were headed back to reality. To a new life I had no clue how to fit into. I knew he would be different when we arrived. Gone would be the doting, loving husband, and in his place, the head of a secret, specialized division that hunted down and eliminated people who caused harm to "innocents," as Matteo called them.

I had felt his removal from me as soon as we boarded the plane. He sat across from me, the farthest we'd been apart in two weeks. Conversation ceased almost immediately, and soon, he was immersed in work.

I knew he expected me to join him in his fight. To work with his family members to make sure the money they absorbed went to fighting child porn rings, breaking up sex slave operations, and helping people they had rescued. I wasn't sure I would be able to handle it or even how I would fit in. I was a stranger. Matteo's wife, but still an outsider to all his people. I had to learn how to be Evie Campari instead of Evelyn Harper. The wife of a powerful, dangerous man. I had to find my place in his world, but I wasn't even sure how to begin to do so.

Would his men, his sister, accept me? Would I let him down?

"Evie."

His voice startled me out of my thoughts, and I looked at him. His work was gone, and he sat, one leg crossed over the other, regarding me as if he was waiting for a response.

"Yes, Matteo. I'm sorry. I must have missed what you were saying."

"I asked where you were."

Confused, I offered him a smile. "I'm right here."

Uncrossing his legs, he leaned forward, brushing back a strand of hair from my face. "No, Evie, you are a thousand miles outside this plane, stuck in some dark place in your head. I'd like you to come back and talk to me."

"I was letting you work."

He nodded, his fingers still soothing their way up and down my cheek. "I appreciate that, but I stopped over twenty minutes ago. I've been sitting here, watching you, and wondering why my wife is so terrified that she is destroying her clothing."

I looked down in shock. He was right; I was gripping the material of my skirt so hard, I had torn the seam. If that wasn't enough, my fingers had worried the fabric so much it was broken down and frayed.

"I'm so sorry. I didn't mean——"

"Evie!"

His sharp tone stopped my words. They dried up in my throat as I stared at him, fear spiking down my spine.

He cupped my face, shaking his head. "Do not look at me with fear, beautiful girl. You need *never* fear me. I love you, and you are my world."

Tears filled my eyes, and with a groan, he undid my seat belt and pulled me onto his lap. He wrapped his arms around me and pressed kisses to my head.

I inhaled deeply, his scent calming me. In his arms, there was no fear or worry. Only him, only us.

"I'm sorry, Evie. I know this is all still new and frightening to you. I hadn't meant to work on the flight home, but Julian sent me some files I had to go through right away. Otherwise, I would disappear when we arrived home, and I wanted our first night at the house spent together."

"It's fine," I whispered.

"Tell me what is upsetting you so much."

I leaned my head back, meeting his gaze. His deep brown eyes were soft and concerned—there was no anger or judgment. *My* Matteo was here.

"I worry I will disappoint you. That I will step out of line and cause you embarrassment. I worry I won't be able to handle working with your sister, or she won't like me. She never came near me the night we married or since then. What—what if I do something to displease you?"

Matteo frowned. "I fully expect you to—I'll do the same to you. Evie, what do you think I am? Do you think I would harm a hair on your head? Do you think I'm some sort of monster?" He cupped my cheek. "I'm just a man. A man in love with his wife. Nothing is going to happen. We might argue. If I get angry, we'll get through it. If I anger you, the same thing. Couples fight." He ran a finger under my eyes, wiping away my tears. "Gianna will come around. She's incredibly nervous of new people, but she will warm to you. Let her do it on her own time. She will come to you when she is ready. As for the rest, I will help you. Roza and Lila will be there to help you as well. And if you hate that aspect, then you can do something else." He tweaked my nose. "I need lunch daily, and you told me you loved to bake. You know I have a sweet tooth."

"You…we—we won't be the same."

"As we were on the island?"

"Yes."

"Yes and no. Will I sweep you into my arms and kiss you in front of my team? Tease and chase you around? No. But nor will I ignore you. You are my wife, and as such, you deserve respect. I am intensely private, and my feelings for you—the deep, unshakable ones—will be between us. But if you need me? If you need my arms or my touch? All you have to do is come to see me. Close my door and tell me privately. Anything you want is yours."

He paused, looking down at me, then bent his head and brushed his lips over mine. "I show only strength to my team, Evie. Although some are family, I am still their boss. They don't get the private side of Matteo unless I allow it—which is rare. But you, my wife, you get all of me. When I'm conducting business, I do what I have to in order to maintain my role, but in private, I am yours. My heart is always with you, even when I'm somewhere else. Don't allow the façade I have to use make you think anything else." He dropped another kiss to my mouth. "Never forget what you mean to me. You can always talk to me. I want to know what you're thinking and feeling."

His lips quirked. "Unless, of course, I'm in a meeting and you decide right then to yell at me about missing the hamper with my socks."

A little giggle escaped my lips. He smiled back at me, then became serious.

"What I do is dangerous, Evie. It's one of the reasons I never thought I would get married. I didn't want to endanger anyone. I had no soft spot for anyone to take advantage of—to use against me. But you changed that. My biggest fear is that it become known how profoundly in love with you I am and you become a target because of me. What I do, what my team does, is kept under such tight wraps that only a handful of people know for sure we are real. There is gossip and rumors, but nothing that leads to me directly. I want to keep it that way, now more than ever. And I will take every precaution."

"So, when it's business or in public, you'll be removed?"

"Yes. I have to be in order to protect you. To protect us." He studied me. "Can you handle that? Knowing I'm doing it for your safety?"

"When we're alone?"

"I will be close. Just be aware of our surroundings when there are other people." He grimaced. "As I discovered with Frank, there are those who cannot be trusted."

"I understand."

"Yet you still look so sad."

"I like holding your hand and kissing you whenever I like." I smiled sadly. "I guess I got used to that."

"You can hold my hand. I can keep you close to me. That would seem natural in my world. But the kissing, no. Any form of public affection."

"Will you make it up to me?"

He lowered his face. "Every chance I get."

"Okay, then."

"Ready to join the real world?"

"As long as you're with me."

He held me closer. "I am *always* with you, Evie. My heart is yours."

The house bustled with activity when we arrived. I made sure to follow Matteo's cues when we left the plane. He offered me his hand to help me descend the steps and again to get into the car, then I waited while he spoke with the driver. When he slid in beside me, he lifted my hand to his lips with murmured praise. "That's my girl."

Geo and Lila were on hand to greet us when we got home, hugging us. Geo nodded, satisfied with what he saw. "You look well, Evie."

I met Matteo's amused glance and smiled. "I am."

"We brought dinner, so you wouldn't have to worry about it."

"Where is Mrs. Armstrong?" Matteo asked, looking around the empty kitchen.

Geo frowned. "She had a heart attack two days ago, Matteo."

"What? Why was I not informed?"

"She's fine and resting comfortably. She begged me not to ruin your time away. She told me you never relax enough, and she wanted you to be gone as long as possible with your little angel. I agreed to abide by her wishes since you were returning today and she was doing so well."

"We should go and see her, Matteo," I said. Mrs. Armstrong had always been kind to me.

"Yes. Once we're unpacked and settled. Is she getting private care? Is there anything she needs?"

"I made sure she had the best of everything. She won't be back to work for a while, and even then, it will be restricted."

"I'll have to hire a new housekeeper."

I laid a hand on his arm. "No, I'll take care of the house, Matteo."

He frowned. "I don't want you doing chores, Evie."

I laughed. "Mrs. Armstrong has a crew that does the chores weekly—she oversees them. But I can do the cooking and shopping. And if she comes back, I can help her." I beseeched him with my eyes. "I would like to look after my husband in that way."

His eyes glittered in the light, and he bent low. "You will be well rewarded for it, my wife."

I bit my lip and tried not to notice the grins on Geo's and Lila's faces.

"I look forward to it."

CHAPTER NINE

Evie

Dinner was enjoyable, and I began to relax. Matteo was nowhere near as affectionate, but he was still close. And I knew once we were alone, the tender side of him would be out in full force. I hoped the demanding, possessive side would make an appearance as well.

He and Geo slipped away after dinner for a fast chat, and Lila and I put away the leftovers and sipped some coffee.

"Matteo looks very happy. As do you."

"I am. I hope he is too. I want him happy. He deserves that," I added softly.

She regarded me with a wide smile. "You love him."

"Yes."

"And he has finally found love with someone—you."

I traced my finger on the dark wood of the table. "Yes," I responded. "He does love me."

"I'm thrilled. I know it's not an easy life he lives, Evie, but with you in it, he will find some peace and happiness. That has been missing for far too long."

"Thank you."

"It will take you some time to adjust, but you will be fine. Remember, the man you love has many faces, and although you may not like them all, he is there, no matter what. I believe Matteo will be a good husband to you."

"I think so as well."

Leaning forward, she patted my hand. "If there is anything I can do to help, let me know. I remember how overwhelming all this was when I married Geo. I knew what I was getting into, yet at times, it threatened to overwhelm me. This has all been thrust upon you."

"How did you handle it?"

"I trusted him. I learned how to separate the two lives and be what he needed me to be in both of them. He had to adjust his way of thinking as well, so we learned together." She chuckled. "We had many spectacular arguments—and some very intense make-up times afterward."

I joined in her amusement. Then I became serious.

"Matteo worries about my safety. That I could become a liability to him."

She nodded. "They all fear that instance. Vince, Alex, Geo. I would imagine, given Matteo's position, it would be even more so. Follow his lead, listen to what he asks, and you'll be fine."

"He was hoping I would work with you."

"We would love that. It's very rewarding to see what we can do for those who truly need it. An extra pair of hands is always welcome." She stood. "You concentrate on your marriage and the house for the next while. I can help you find your way around, and we can talk about it more later on. You can talk to Roza and Gianna, and then decide."

She picked up her cup. "You look tired. Go and finish unpacking. I will get Geo and send Matteo up as soon as possible. I'm sure he hates being away from you—even for a short while."

I smiled sadly. I knew I couldn't have him all the time anymore. "Time to get back to reality."

She hugged me, her soft, floral scent surrounding me, reminding me of a mother's gentle hug.

"All will be fine. I promise."

I headed upstairs, hoping she was right.

Matteo entered our room, smiling at me. "What are you doing?"

"Unpacking and sorting laundry for tomorrow."

"Mrs. Armstrong will…" He caught himself. "Are you sure you don't want me to hire someone?"

"I am perfectly capable of doing laundry."

He came up behind me, settling his hands on my hips, pulling me back to his chest. "I am aware of how capable you are, my beauty." He slid his hands up my torso, cupping my breasts, teasing my nipples gently. He dropped his face to my neck, his breath warm on my skin. "I'm aware of you…*everything* about you."

I let my head fall back, granting him free access to my neck. "Oh?" I whimpered.

"I'm aware you had a shower without me. I'm aware you're wearing one of the sexiest little nightgowns I have ever seen in my life." His hands tugged at the hem of the lacy garment. "I'm aware right now you don't give a flying fuck about the laundry, the housework, or anything else but me throwing you on the bed, *our bed*, and fucking you." He sucked at the juncture of my neck, making me gasp as he bit down.

"Is that a fact?" I murmured, trying desperately to maintain some sort of control. I tried not to groan as he pulled me tight to him, the evidence of his desire hard against my ass.

With a low laugh, he gathered my nightgown higher. "I'm aware—" his breathing became deeper "—that you have nothing on under here." He cupped me, his touch possessive. "I'm aware how much you want me. Right now."

I whimpered.

Without warning, he inserted two fingers inside, curling them to hit the spot that drove me crazy. I cried out as he started pumping them quickly. I arched into his touch, my orgasm coming hard and fast. Before I had even recovered, he threw me onto the bed, standing over me with a wicked grin as he tugged his shirt over his head and tore off his pants. In seconds, he was on me, his mouth everywhere, kissing, teasing, licking, and caressing. He touched me, his hands ghosting over my skin, leaving a trail of heat behind. He hovered over me, his breathing ragged, his eyes hooded and dark.

"How is it possible to have missed you in such a short time span? How can my body crave you so constantly?"

I cupped his cheek at his sweet words. He turned his head, kissing my palm.

"You are everything to me, Evie. I should fear the power you hold over me."

"I feel the same way, Matteo. You mean more than I can express."

He lowered his face to mine and kissed me. The urgency built between us again, the passion flaring as our mouths touched. He slid inside me, groaning as our bodies merged, moving as one. He buried his face in my neck, kissing the skin.

"So sweet. You always taste so sweet here," he whispered. "You smell so good—like light and sunshine. Like home."

I pulled his head back to mine, and our mouths fused. He moved faster, claiming me with his touch and body. I cried out as another orgasm hit me, and he moaned my name as he stiffened, his cock throbbing with his release.

For a moment, there was silence. Then he lifted his head, hovering over me. "Welcome home, Mrs. Campari."

I smiled up at him. "I love you."

His face lit up, wonder and happiness filling his eyes.

"I love you."

Matteo was quiet during breakfast, already turning on boss mode. I was beginning to recognize the signs. His shoulders would draw back, and his eyes would shutter, becoming emotionless. I didn't like it, but I realized it was his cover.

He drained his mug and stood. "What are your plans this morning?"

"I need to make a grocery list, go shopping, and figure out Mrs. Armstrong's schedule."

"Marcus will drive you to the grocery store."

I frowned. "Is that necessary? I know how to drive, and I can read a map."

"It is necessary."

"Mrs. Armstrong went to the store on her own. It seems a waste of Marcus's time to accompany me shopping. I'm sure he has more important things to take care of for you."

He leaned on the counter, boxing me in. His voice was low, his gaze fierce, the boss gone and my husband firmly in my face. "Mrs. Armstrong is not my wife. There is *nothing* more important than your safety. *Nothing.* Marcus accompanies you, or you don't go. Am I clear?"

"Yes."

His kiss was hard. "Good."

For a moment, he stared at me, his fingers on my cheek. Then his mask came down, and he straightened and left the kitchen.

I tidied up, checked the contents of the cupboards, fridge, and freezer, then made my list. Mrs. Armstrong kept the pantry well stocked, but there were a few things I wanted to add. It would take me a while to figure out the flow of the kitchen, but I was looking forward to it. My mom had died when I was young, and my dad had been hopeless when it came to cooking. I'd taken over and always enjoyed cooking and baking. I found it relaxing, and I was good at it. It was the only thing Blaine didn't criticize about me.

I shook my head. I wasn't going to spare him another thought. Ever. He didn't deserve my thoughts or sympathy.

Instead, I racked my brain to think of the recipe for my double chocolate brownie cookies. Matteo would love them. I looked over to the desk by the window and the old laptop sitting on it. Sitting down, I opened the lid and stared at the screen. Of course it needed a username and password. I knew neither. I hadn't asked Matteo for internet access, the thought never crossing my mind with everything else. I began to close the lid, accidentally pushing the laptop away, and I noticed a small piece of paper under the laptop. Curious, I pulled it out, grinning at what I found.

Camparikitchen/Pastanoodles123 was written in old-fashioned cursive, a bold underline under the C and P to remind herself to capitalize the letters, no doubt. I recognized Mrs. Armstrong's writing. I opened up the laptop again and tried the information, smiling in delight when it worked. Remembering the website I liked, I typed in the address, and while I waited for it to do its thing, I searched for another piece of paper in the drawer. Finally, the recipe came up, and I scribbled it down, adding a couple more items to my list.

Marcus came into the kitchen and watched me for a moment. "Found Mrs. Armstrong's hidden password?" he asked, surprising me by speaking.

"Yes. I needed to look at a recipe I wanted to make later on a site I used to use all the time."

He furrowed his brow.

"I didn't try to access my old account. I went in as a guest. I have no email to set up a new one." I couldn't help my sigh. "Shame. I had so many good recipes in that old account."

"What was your old account listed under?"

"Baker2.0 at hotmail," I said. "I loved collecting cookie recipes."

His face cleared. "Are you ready to go then, Mrs. Campari?"

I hesitated, then picked up my purse. "I need to see Matteo before I leave."

He nodded, indicating to follow him. At the door of Matteo's office on the other side of the house, he knocked and waited until Matteo shouted out for him to enter.

"Mrs. Campari wishes a moment."

"Of course. Give us the room."

I slipped inside, and Marcus shut the door behind me. Matteo sat at his huge desk, computers and files surrounding him. He already looked exhausted. However, he smiled at me, his expression welcoming.

"Hello, my wife."

I approached the desk, unsure how to ask my question.

"Once again, your possessions are suffering from your nerves," he observed.

I looked down at my purse. I was wringing the handle.

He stood and rounded the desk, leaning on it, then opening his arms. "Come to me."

I stepped forward, and he embraced me, holding me tight. "What is it, *Piccolina?*"

"I-I'm not sure how to pay for the groceries, and I have no money…"

"Evie, I apologize." He dropped a kiss on my head and lifted my chin. "I meant to discuss that with you last evening, but I was, ah, distracted." He nipped the end of my nose playfully, then went back to his desk and rummaged in the top drawer. He pulled out an envelope.

"Here are your new bank cards. Your password is the date of our marriage." He stated the numbers slowly. "There is a Visa card, a debit card, and your account will be replenished as needed." He pulled a thick envelope from another drawer and withdrew some bills, offering them to me. "Here's five hundred dollars."

I gaped at him, and he frowned. "Is that not enough? You have ten thousand in your account, but if you need more—"

I shook my head, aghast. "Matteo, I wanted twenty dollars and some money for groceries."

He chuckled and came to me, sliding the money and cards into my wallet. "That is not your life anymore. Buy what you think we need and, most importantly, anything you *want*."

I looked at my fat wallet. "Is there anything *you* want?"

"I want you home and safe." He grinned. "And perhaps some cookies, if you have time later."

"I already planned on that."

His kiss was long and possessive. "Good, my wife. That is good."

The drive was silent, the area unfamiliar. Once we left the large estate, I lost track of the turns, but I was surprised when we pulled onto a major road in a short time period.

"I thought we were right in the country."

Marcus kept his eyes on the road. "No, we're not far from all the suburban necessities, but far enough away it feels open. Mr. Campari owns a lot of land around your home. He, ah, likes the privacy."

Coming as I did from Alberta, a lot of the stores were unfamiliar to me, but I recognized the name of the grocery chain Marcus drove us to. Eager to do something normal, I flung open the door and began to walk as soon as he'd stopped the car. He made a sound of distress, catching up with me and touching my elbow.

"Mrs. Campari, it is my job to keep you safe. Please remain in the car until I have assessed the situation and opened the door for you. Mr. Campari wants me at your side at all times."

"Assessed the situation? Do you think someone is going to grab me in the grocery store parking lot?" I asked, teasing.

His face darkened, and all he said was one word. "Please."

I sobered and nodded, slowing my pace. I had to remind myself I was living a different life now.

In the store, we were quiet as I perused the aisles. As I looked at the packages of pasta, Marcus shook his head. "Mr. Campari prefers homemade pasta."

Surprised by his words, I smiled. "I don't know how to make fresh pasta."

"I can show you. Mrs. Armstrong has the pasta maker. I taught her as well."

"Okay. I'd like that."

"I didn't mean to frighten you earlier, Mrs. Campari. I'm following orders, and I know how much…" He paused. "I know how important it is to Mr. Campari."

"I understand. May I ask you something?"

"Of course."

"Do you call my husband Mr. Campari to his face?"

"No."

"Then call me Evie. Please."

He hesitated, then offered me a smile. He was a good-looking man—a few years older than Matteo, I judged. Dark hair and eyes, he could be related to him. He was broader than Matteo and a few inches taller and muscular. His expression was serious, but if you looked closely enough, his eyes held a softness within their dark depths.

"Evie, then. I would be happy to show you how to make pasta."

"I would enjoy that. Thank you, Marcus." I beamed up at him.

He returned my smile. "Mr. Campari, ah, Matteo, doesn't like nuts in his cookies." He paused. "Neither do I."

"That makes three of us."

"Okay."

The rest of the shopping excursion, he pointed out Matteo's favorites, and we discussed recipes. He told me his parents had owned a restaurant and he'd practically grown up in the kitchen. After we loaded the car, he opened the door, and I slipped into the passenger seat.

"Could we go to the mall?"

He paused. "Matteo said the store, then home."

"I need a few personal things. Maybe you could call him?"

"Is it important?"

"To me, yes."

"To the mall, then. But I ask you stay close and be as quick as possible."

"I can do that."

"Thank you, Mrs.——"

I lifted my eyebrow. "We established this, Marcus. Evie. My name is Evie."

He studied me for a moment, then smiled.

"Okay, Evie. To the mall."

CHAPTER TEN

Evie

I made Matteo and Marcus each a sandwich when I got home and sent them to the office with Marcus, waving off his offer to help me unpack the groceries. I had hoped Matteo would bring his plate and come eat in the kitchen, but I knew he was busy since it was his first day back after our honeymoon.

It seemed odd to miss someone who was just down the hall, yet I did.

I was still unpacking the groceries when Alex came in, smiling and carrying a file box.

"Hello, Evie."

"Um, hello."

I watched, horrified, as he took the laptop on the desk, disconnecting it and packing it away.

"I only used it the one time," I protested. "I didn't do anything wrong."

He frowned and shook his head. "Of course you didn't. Matteo asked me to bring a newer, faster machine and a little printer for you." He held up an iPad, and in minutes, he had the printer attached and checked to make sure everything worked. "I set up an email account for you and transferred all your recipes to your new account on the site you were using earlier."

"How did you do that?"

He winked. "Better not to ask."

"Oh. Of course."

He leaned against the desk. "You can surf the net, do anything you want, but no Facebook or social media accounts. No pictures."

"I understand."

"If there is something you want ordered online, please give the information to Matteo. It will be done, delivered to a safe location, and brought to you when it arrives."

I highly doubted I would need anything, but I nodded.

"I made the username and password the same as Mrs. Armstrong had. She rarely ever used it. Change the password if you want."

"Should I tell someone if I do?"

He laughed. "No. We don't monitor the usage, Evie. Marcus mentioned you wishing you had your recipe book from that site, so I got that for you. Matteo thought a printer would be helpful for your recipes. That's all."

"Okay, thank you."

"Anything else you need?"

"Can I use the Kindle app on that?" I asked hopefully.

"Yes." He scribbled something on a piece of paper. "Use this email to open it and the credit card Matteo gave you to purchase the books."

With a wave, he left. He seemed nice enough. I knew he was a cousin of Matteo's. He was tall and slim, once again the Italian heritage showing with the dark hair and eyes. He and Roza made a good-looking couple.

I sat down, tracing the edge of the iPad. It was a sleek, top-of-the-line model—nicer than anything I had ever used before. I looked forward to trying it. Reading. Blaine hated it when I read. He felt as if I was ignoring him. He wanted my attention focused on him at all times.

I lifted my hand to my cheek, recalling the first time he'd hit me. I'd been reading and missed something he said. The next thing I knew, my Kindle was in pieces on the floor and my head rang from the slap across the face I'd received. The pain and shock had rendered me useless, and he had shaken me, screaming in my face about my priorities. It was the beginning of the nightmare my life became.

"Evie?" a quiet voice prompted.

I looked up, startled. "Matteo." I stood. "I'm sorry I didn't hear you come in."

"I came to see if the tablet was acceptable. I thought you would like it." He studied me. "Perhaps I was mistaken?"

"What?" I wiped my eyes. "Oh no, it's lovely."

"Why, then, are you crying? Did Alex say something that upset you? He said you thought you'd done something wrong, but that wasn't why I was changing the equipment."

"No, not at all."

"Tell me," he demanded, then tempered his voice and took my hand. "Please."

Unable to look at him, I explained my memory.

His grip tightened on me, then he wrapped me in his arms. "*Piccolina*, I'm sorry. For all you went through." He sighed. "For how we came to be. But you are here with me now and safe." He pulled me closer. "He is dead now, Evie. You need never fear him again."

My body jerked at his words. "Dead?" I whispered.

"Yes."

"Did you—did you…?"

He sighed.

"No." He eased back, lifting up my chin. "I had planned to, but he did it on his own. He pissed off another prisoner and was killed in a fight."

"Oh." A tremor went through me.

"This upsets you?" he asked, incredulous. "After all he did to you, you still have mercy for him?"

"No. It's just a shock, I suppose. Maybe some relief?" I replied, unsure how to explain how I was feeling.

"You will never be touched in anger again. I swear this to you."

"I know," I murmured, nestling close, the fear fading and calm settling in my chest.

Was that what I needed? Matteo's arms?

"I'm always safe with you."

"You are. With me. In this house. Out with Marcus. You will always be safe."

He pressed his lips to my head, holding me until Marcus's voice spoke behind him.

"Matteo, Julian is on the line, waiting."

"I'll be right there."

He pulled away and cupped my face. "Enough of the past. Make me some cookies, my wife. And a list of everything you want. A stereo for in here? New cookie trays? A bigger desk? Whatever you want, it is yours."

He nodded decisively and headed to the door to follow Marcus. He glanced over his shoulder. "I'll be back to check on the cookie-making progress later." He winked, making me smile, then he was gone.

With it, he took the bad memories that had appeared. He gave me something to do—asked me for something.

I had cookies to make.

Three hours later, the kitchen smelled like a bakery. Cookies of all sorts filled the containers on the counter. I'd found an old radio and turned it on, the music helping me feel more at home in the kitchen that still felt as if it belonged to someone else.

The kitchen door opened, and Matteo strode in, smiling.

"All I can smell is cookies."

"I made your favorites. A little birdie gave me the lowdown."

He peeked into the containers with a grin. "Marcus?"

"Maybe."

He laughed and grabbed a few, munching away happily. I poured him a coffee, and he sat down and sipped, looking thoughtful.

"You also went to the mall earlier."

"I needed a couple of things. I was quick."

He sighed. "I'm not upset. I don't want you to feel like a prisoner, but I want to be cautious."

"I know." I hesitated. "Do Roza and Lila have, ah, protection?"

"Both Roza and Lila carry guns and know how to defend themselves."

"Oh. And Gianna?"

"Gianna never leaves the property without Vince, Marcus, or me. Ever. That's her choice, by the way. After what happened to her, she is unable to bear the thought of being out in the world on her own."

"So, should I carry a gun?"

The cookie he was eating stopped midway to his mouth, and he grimaced. "I'm not comfortable with the thought of you having a gun. Unless you've had training in firearms?"

"No. Maybe some martial arts training would make you feel better—I could take someone down?"

"Take someone down?" he repeated, his lips quirking.

I nodded. "Or self-defense courses?"

He groaned and stood. "Can we discuss this at another date?" He studied me. "Are you so anxious to get away from me already you need to escape, no matter what?"

I stepped close, cupping his face. "No. I simply don't want to be a burden. I hate to think if we run out of milk, I need to drag Marcus away from his work."

"For now, that is how it has to be." He chuckled. "Besides, I believe you have a fan in Marcus." He shook his head. "My hardened right-hand adores you, I think. You weave your spell and entrap us all, Evie."

"I only want to entrap you."

"You have. For the first time ever, I cannot concentrate on my responsibilities. It's as if I can sense where you are in the house, and I want to be with you."

"Matteo," I breathed out.

He cupped my face, kissing me hard. "My temptress, my wife."

I leaned into his embrace, feeling content.

He stood back, brushing off his pants. "I must leave you, but I look forward to dinner."

"Eight?"

He nodded. "Eight o'clock." He reached for another handful of cookies. "These will keep me going until then."

He left the kitchen, his absence making the room seem foreign and empty once more.

I shook my head at my thoughts. I only had to get used to my new surroundings.

I was certain it would feel like home soon.

It had to.

The next morning, I woke to find Matteo gone, but on his pillow was a small box. I sat up, opening it to find a stunning pair of diamond earrings. Simple studs, not too large, but beautiful. I slipped them in, looking at my reflection in the mirror. I hardly recognized myself. My hair was a mass of different colors, some due to the skill of the hairdresser Matteo arranged to come see me, some from the time in the sun. My skin glowed, and the exhaustion I had lived with so long faded from under my eyes. The diamonds I wore glittered at my ears and on my finger. As simple as the clothes I wore looked, I was certain they cost a fortune.

Donning my swimsuit, I headed downstairs. In the pool, I swam some laps, enjoying the exercise and the way the water felt flowing over my body. I noticed the noodles and the new floating lounger waiting in the corner and spent a little while relaxing in it as I thought about what to do today. I had never been in a position to do nothing before. I went to school, I worked, then I looked after my dad and, finally, Blaine, who had never-ending lists of chores for me every day. Now I had all the time in the world, and I wasn't sure how to fill it.

Eventually, I got out, dried off, and headed upstairs. I showered and dressed, then went to the kitchen. I made coffee and poured a cup, sitting at the desk and perusing the new machine. I checked my account on the recipe site, pleased to see all the files I had saved over the years. I printed one for pasta e fagioli soup, deciding that would make an easy dinner later. Remembering I had bought yeast yesterday, I spent some time making a batch of bread, thinking that would go well with the soup.

Restless and unable to settle, I headed to the great room and looked out at the sky. Overhead, it was sunny, although there were some clouds on the horizon. I opened the door and headed outside, walking around the gardens. I knew he would rather I have Marcus with me when I went outside, but it seemed unnecessary.

I waved at Lila, who smiled and waved back through the window in the office she worked from. I hadn't gone to see her there yet. I needed a little more time. I stopped and deadheaded some plants in the garden, eyeing a nice spot that would work for herbs. I would ask Matteo later if I could add to the garden area. I explored the large yard, stopping to appreciate the pool and entertaining area, wondering if it was ever used. I pulled some weeds from the planters, sat on one of the padded chairs for a while, then kept exploring. I admired the house set back in the trees where Vince and Gianna lived. It was modern and simple, but it looked welcoming, with plants marking the pathway and a cheerful wreath hanging on the door. I headed toward the trees, delighted when I found a gazebo with wide benches and a vine-covered roof. Roses grew up the sides, mingled with ivy, making it pretty. Beside it was a small brook that bubbled in the most pleasant fashion. I sat down, pulling my legs up to my chest, enjoying the fragrant surroundings. It was peaceful, beautiful, and I decided it was my favorite spot on the property. I shut my eyes, enjoying the stillness, and drifted with no thoughts except to appreciate the moment.

"Evie."

Startled, I lifted my head, finding Matteo leaning against the gazebo, watching me. He had an indulgent smile on his face, but his eyes were serious.

"Matteo."

He came in and sat beside me, taking my hand. "You disappeared from sight, my wife."

I blinked. "You were watching me?"

He smiled. "How could I not? I saw you wandering the grounds—" he lifted his eyebrows "—*unaccompanied*, exploring. I saw you in the gardens, looking at the pool, pulling weeds, then suddenly, I couldn't see you anymore."

"I need to be accompanied even in the yard?" I hated the idea of being followed around all the time.

He sighed. "No, but I would like to know if you're leaving the house. Alex said you'd headed this way, so I came to find you. I don't like not knowing where you are."

"How did Alex know?"

"We monitor the grounds at all times, Evie. I can see you through the windows or a camera feed on my computer. But there isn't one here. That's the issue."

I felt a flash of disappointment. "But it's so lovely here, Matteo. The water and the gazebo. Don't tell me I can't come sit here. Please."

He took my hand, kissing my wrist and holding it to his chest. "I can't deny you anything, Evie. Of course you can come sit here. You're safe on the grounds, although it distressed Marcus as well when you disappeared from view." He glanced around. "But we'll solve that issue easily."

I knew that meant the next time I came here, a camera would watch over me. Somehow it spoiled it a little for me, but I knew arguing wouldn't help. Matteo made the rules, and he wouldn't change his mind.

He leaned closer, touching my ear, his thumb rubbing the soft skin and making me shiver. "I see you got my gift."

"They're beautiful."

"As are you. I want to surround you in beauty."

He leaned forward, capturing my mouth. His kiss stole my senses, making me long for more. He pulled me to his lap, his tongue and lips working mine, making me forget everything around me.

When he eased back, he tucked me under his chin.

"You can't do that if you put a camera here," I said, sounding breathless.

He laughed, tilting up my chin and kissing my nose. "Ah, how you underestimate me. I'll control the camera and turn it off when I come to see you."

"I see."

"You're upset."

I hesitated, then decided to be honest. "I hate thinking I'm watched all the time. I never know when Marcus will appear—or you, even. I'm not leaving the grounds. I'm not trying to leave the grounds. I'm just looking around. You say you want me to feel at home here, but I can't relax, not totally, thinking my every move is monitored."

He was quiet for a moment, looking contemplative.

"I'll ask Marcus to ease off. There are cameras all around the perimeter, so I suppose adding more is overkill."

"Do you not trust me?"

He shook his head. "That isn't it at all."

I waited for him to finish his thoughts.

He took my hand in his. "I feel this need to watch over you, Evie. To make sure you're okay—to make up for the years you were neglected and hurt." He stopped, his voice lowering. "I've never loved someone this way, and it's making me anxious. What I do has never had such far-reaching consequences until you. My worry is you will be hurt because of me, and I can't find peace unless I know you're safe."

Hearing his quiet confession made my heart race. "I'm sorry," I offered. "I didn't know you felt that way. I don't mean to complain."

"You haven't complained. But we'll compromise. I won't put up a camera here. You can be alone here with your thoughts and curse me out if you're angry, and I'll be none the wiser. Just stay away from the brook. I don't want you falling in."

I leaned forward and kissed him. "Thank you."

He was quiet for a moment. "Evie, I have a dinner to attend later this week. As part of my cover, I have to go to these functions on occasion. I would like you to accompany me."

"All right."

"Roza will get you a dress. She'll come to see you later."

"Couldn't I go with her to pick one out?"

I felt him tense up, and I ran my fingers over his jaw. "I would like to pick my own dress. It's just the mall."

"I cannot spare anyone tomorrow."

"You said she carries a gun. I wouldn't leave her sight. Please."

I felt his indecision. He swallowed. "I'll arrange it."

I cupped his face and drew him back to my mouth. "Thank you."

I decided not to push my luck, and we walked back to the house, side by side, our fingers entwined.

"Matteo, what is that room for?" I asked, pointing to the windows of the small space I had looked at the other day.

"Nothing. I think the architect called it an extra study." He glanced down. "Did you want it, Evie?"

"Can I? I would love a space to craft."

He frowned. "Craft? What is that?"

"Make things. Do some sewing. Make a wreath for the front door. Decorate pinecones at Christmas. A place I can go and make a mess and not have to clean up."

He threw back his head in laughter. "You want a wreath for the front door? You could buy one."

"But making it would be fun. I was hoping maybe Gianna, Roza, or Lila might enjoy it as well. I love making things with my hands."

He pulled me in for a fast hug as we got to the doors of the great room. "Then make a list of what you want, and we'll make you a space to, ah, 'craft.'"

In the house, he looked down at me. "You are full of little surprises, Evie. I enjoy discovering all your talents." He bent and kissed me. "Try to stay out of trouble the rest of the day. It's going to rain later, so stay inside. Plan your room. I'll see you at dinner."

"Did you want lunch?"

"No, I'll be out most of the day. I'm meeting with Julian."

"All right."

He ran his fingers over my cheek, then strode away. I headed to the kitchen to check on the bread. After, I was going to the little space to do some measuring. I had a room to plan.

The next morning, I woke up to find a new Kindle on Matteo's pillow. There was a note with all the information, plus the email address and a two-year prepaid Kindle Unlimited subscription, as well as a five-hundred-dollar gift card in the Amazon account.

For my beloved,
For your beloved
(books, that is)

Matteo

I shook my head in wonder. He remembered everything I said. When I'd told him about Blaine hitting me, I had mentioned the Kindle and how I had missed it when it broke. This one was brand-new, top-of-the-line, with a beautiful cover and tons of memory. My other one had been old, and most of the time, I'd just downloaded free books—especially once Blaine had his hooks into me. When it broke, I knew there was no chance of replacing it.

But Matteo did.

I got up and dressed, hurrying through my routine. I headed downstairs, going directly to Matteo's office. The door was closed, but I heard his voice, and I knocked. Marcus opened the door, lifting his eyebrows in surprise.

"He's on the phone, Evie. Is something the matter?"

I shook my head. "Please ask him to come see me. I'll only take a moment of his time."

He smiled. "I'm sure he'll have more than a moment to spare for you."

I went to the kitchen and made coffee, turning as the door opened and Matteo strode in. His shirt sleeves were rolled up, and he hadn't shaved today. His hair was brushed off his forehead but not slicked back. He looked sexy, slightly rumpled, and completely intense.

"Evie, what is it?"

I lunged, throwing my arms around him and pressing my mouth to his. It took him a second to react, then he slid his hands under my ass, yanking me tight and kissing me back with a fiery passion. He sat me on the counter, sliding his hands up my neck and cupping my head, slanting his mouth firmly onto mine. I wrapped my legs around his hips, and I felt his erection grow as our mouths moved and caressed. He broke away, breathing hard.

"Evie." He whispered my name. "What has gotten into you?"

"You," I replied, kissing along his scruff. "You, Matteo. I want you."

With a low growl, he jerked me closer, running his hand up my leg and under the skirt I had worn.

"Jesus, you're bare under here." His eyes widened. "And so wet, my wife. You want me."

I yanked on his belt, fumbling with the button on his pants. "Please," I whispered.

He pushed my hands aside, his pants falling to the floor. He spread my thighs and drove into me, making me whimper.

"I don't have much time," he managed to grit out.

"I don't need it," I replied, meeting his powerful strokes. I clung to his shoulders, burying my face into his neck. He gripped my hip with one hand, anchoring us to the counter with the other. He uttered curses in a low voice, growled his pleasure into my ear, and took me hard and fast—exactly the way I wanted. I orgasmed quickly, shaking around him, and he followed not long after, his deep groan muffled in my hair. A long, shaking breath left him, and he leaned heavily on me for a moment, before capturing my face in his hands and kissing me again.

He got dressed quickly, smoothing my skirt down. "I'll be all over you today," he murmured.

I smiled. "Until I go swimming."

"Wait until tonight. I'll swim with you." He tapped my nose. "I like knowing you'll smell like me all day."

"Okay," I replied, noting how his eyes lit up at my words.

I cupped his cheek. "Thank you for my Kindle."

He smiled, his voice affectionate. "It amuses me that your reaction to the Kindle was far more enthusiastic than the diamonds." He rubbed my earlobe, touching the glittering gems. "You are a special woman, Evie."

"I loved the earrings," I assured him. "This gift seemed more personal somehow."

"If my gifts are going to get this kind of reaction, I'll wake you up before I leave in the morning so you can thank me in the privacy of our room," he said, trying to look stern and failing.

"I'd like it if you woke me, but I don't need a gift."

He studied me for a moment, then kissed me again. This time, his lips were light, sweet, and playful.

"I'll remember that." He smiled. "I'm glad the Kindle made you so happy."

"It did. So do you."

"Then my work here is done—at least for now. I'll come to the library at lunch, and we can eat there, yes?"

"How did you know I'd be there?"

He chuckled. "It's raining out, and I already know your second-favorite place is the chair by the fire. It's cool out, so I had Marcus switch it on. Enjoy your Kindle, and I'll see you later."

"Thank you again."

"It is my greatest joy to make you happy, Evie."

I watched him leave, thinking how empty the room seemed once he'd left.

The next morning, Matteo was there when I woke, and my gift was him. Naked, passionate, and hungry for me. It was my favorite gift of all.

After, we showered, and as I was getting dressed, he studied me in the mirror.

"You look lovely."

I glanced down at the skirt I was wearing. I loved how pretty I felt in the clothes Roza picked for me, but I wanted to choose a few things on my own. Including the dress I needed for tomorrow night.

As if reading my mind, Matteo sighed and met my gaze. "Roza and Lila will take you shopping this afternoon. Julian insists on a meeting with all of us, and I have no time this morning."

I felt the flutter of excitement, but I remained calm.

"All right."

"You get a dress, and you come home. That is an order, not a request."

I nodded.

"I don't like it," he said. "I want to send someone else with you, but I've been told by a couple of people I'm being overbearing."

I bit my lip, wondering who dared say that to him.

"To the world, you are the wife of a successful businessman. You and I know different. But as Marcus pointed out, outside my very tight circle, no one else does. He agreed that you need some normalcy. So, I am allowing this."

"It'll be fine, Matteo. It's just shopping."

"Apparently you are getting pedicures as well. Roza has arranged it."

I tamped down my delight and nodded.

He tugged on a jacket, smoothing down the sleeves. He stopped and kissed me, his mouth lingering. "Do your shopping and come home."

Then he left.

CHAPTER ELEVEN

Evie

The house felt odd without Matteo and his team in it. There were men outside and one in the large room at the other end of the house, but it felt bigger—emptier. I smiled as Roza came into the kitchen, a small frown on her face.

"Lila is ill."

"What?"

"One of her migraines hit her unexpectedly. Geo is coming to get her." She worried her lip. "I'm not sure Matteo would be happy with just us going."

I frowned in disappointment. "We're only going to the mall, right?" I shook my head. "Even Matteo has said the world thinks he is a businessman and I'm his wife. He avoids publicity—even photos. No one is looking for me, Roza. He's just being overprotective." I clasped my hands imploringly. "Please. I want to pick out my own dress."

"Maybe I should call him."

"He's with Julian in a meeting. Don't interrupt. We'll go and come back. I'll tell him later and deal with his displeasure." I knew I would get a stern lecture, but it would be worth it.

"You're right. We'll go."

At the mall, we went directly to her favorite store and quickly found a dress. Soft and flowing, it flattered me with its graceful lines and simple silhouette. It fell to my knees, the sleeves went to my elbows, hiding the scars on my upper arms, and the delicate peach color suited me. We picked shoes and then headed to the small salon located at the end of the mall. As we waited, Roza got a call, her face paling.

"What?" I asked, anxious.

"My mother has had a stroke and been rushed to the hospital," she said, tears glimmering in her eyes.

I gripped her arm. "Oh no."

"I have to go. We need to go."

"No," I gasped. "Roza, you go. I'll get myself home."

Her eyes widened. "I can't do that, Evie. Matteo would be furious."

I lowered my voice. "I'm in a salon. I'll have my pedicure done, call a cab, and go home. I'll explain to Matteo. Everything will be fine. Go to your mother."

She hesitated, obviously torn.

I offered another suggestion. "I'll call Geo as soon as you leave. He'll come and get me."

"Oh, that would work."

"Go," I urged.

"I'll drop your dress off in the morning."

"Fine." I hugged her. "Go."

She hurried away, and the technician called me over. Once I settled in the chair, I dug in my purse, my mouth going dry when I realized I had left my phone in the kitchen, plugged in. Alex had given it to me, with all the right contacts already listed, and I had never had to use it, so I didn't know any numbers. I had no idea how to call Geo, Matteo, or anyone.

I took in a deep breath and relaxed. I would simply go back to Plan A. I knew the address. I could call from the gate and be let in. I had lots of money. I would take a cab and be home before Matteo arrived. I would tell him later, and although he wouldn't be happy, he would admonish me, and that would be that. Maybe he would realize how over the top he was being and let up on his idea I needed security all the time.

I enjoyed having a pedicure, and the salon staff convinced me to have my nails done as well. They looked pretty, all polished and neat, the light color matching my dress. My toenails were bright in a rich rust color, and the technician added some sparkles to the big toe that made me smile. Using my credit card, I paid the bill and hesitated at the door.

For the first time in months, I was alone and free. No Blaine denying me, ordering me around. I had no security at my side, assigned by a worried Matteo. Marcus was great, but he hated shopping, and I always felt I had to hurry. I glanced at my watch. I'd been gone less than two hours. Surely another thirty minutes wouldn't hurt. I could look around the mall, buy a few things for myself, and then I would go home.

I ignored the little voice telling me Matteo would be on the warpath over my decision. Instead, I turned and walked back into the mall.

I flexed my fingers, the bags in my hand getting heavier. I was tired and my feet hurt. I sat down on a bench, shocked when I realized I had been shopping for over two hours. I had forgotten the simple pleasure of window-shopping. I had never experienced the freedom of being able to buy anything I wanted, and I had lost track of time. I glanced at the bags at my feet with a grimace. I had bought a lot of things—including some items for Matteo.

It had felt nice to simply be Evie, shopping and picking out some items for my husband. It gave me a sense of normalcy that my life lacked. Somehow, though, I was sure Matteo wouldn't agree.

I glanced up and noticed a man lounging on a bench across from me. He was playing on his phone, not looking in my direction, but there was something familiar about him. It occurred to me I had seen him through the window of one of the stores as I shopped. And again later.

I swallowed, my throat suddenly thick. Was he following me? Nerves prickled at my skin, and I tried as nonchalantly as possible to pick up my bags and head toward the salon. I would use their phone and call a cab. I walked slowly, peeking in windows, my tension increasing as I realized he was trailing behind me, far enough away I wouldn't normally have noticed, but close enough I knew what was happening.

Matteo had been right.

I picked up my pace and arrived at the salon, smiling at the receptionist.

"Could you call me a cab, please? I think I'm done." I tried to sound normal, but my heart was racing. I needed to get home. Back to the safety of the house and Matteo.

"Ah, there you are."

I spun at the sound of Matteo's voice. He was sitting in the waiting area, his legs crossed, a cup of coffee on the table in front of him. He stood, smoothing down his jacket, his voice light. "I was wondering how much of my money you were going to spend today." He approached me, and despite the easy tone in his voice, his gaze was dark and flinty, his shoulders set back in anger. He was livid. Beyond it, even.

I didn't care. Relief so great swelled in me, and without thinking, I dropped my bags and flung myself into his arms. He was shocked, stiff and unmoving for a moment, then enfolded me into his embrace.

He laughed, knowing we were being watched. "Begging forgiveness already." He lowered his head, looking as if he was kissing my cheek.

"We'll talk about this at home. We're leaving. *Now*," he breathed in my ear.

He bent and picked up the bags. "Thank you for the coffee while I waited for my errant wife." He smiled at the group of women all staring at him. He held out his hand. "Home, Evie."

I looked behind me. The man I had seen was nowhere to be found. Had I imagined him?

I took Matteo's hand, his anger evident in his tight grip. I felt a shiver of fear run up my spine.

Suddenly my impromptu shopping trip seemed like the worst idea I had ever had.

In the car, Matteo was silent, his anger rolling off him in waves. I met Marcus's eyes in the mirror and saw his imperceptible headshake as if warning me to stay quiet.

At the house, Matteo opened the door and waited until I climbed out, not touching me. He took the bags from the trunk and walked upstairs, not waiting for me.

With a sinking heart, I followed him.

In our room, he set down the bags in the closet.

"Matteo," I began.

"Do not speak, Evie."

"You're angry," I breathed.

"No." He shook his head. "I'm furious."

"I'm sorry, I—"

"Sorry for what? Disobeying my direct request you not be out of this house without security? For leaving despite the fact that it was only you and Roza, and then once you were on your own, wandering for hours without contacting Geo as you promised her?"

"How did you know?" I asked quietly.

"I knew Lila had a headache, and because your phone didn't move, I assumed you had the common sense to stay home. When Roza called to tell Alex about her mother, I discovered otherwise."

"My phone didn't move?" I frowned. "What does that mean?"

"All our phones are tracked. Yours never moved from the house. I thought you were here with it. I never imagined you would leave without it on your person."

I should have known Matteo could trace my phone. No doubt he could trace anything he wanted to.

"I forgot it."

"You forgot a lot of things today. Including your promise to me."

I felt my cheeks flush at his words, but I ignored them. "So, you came to the mall."

"Yes. Marcus convinced me not to go in there and drag you out. I let one of my men stay close, and I waited for you. I assumed you would go back to the salon to get them to call a cab for you."

"You did?"

"There are no phone booths in the mall, Evie. It was only logical."

"So, the man I saw—he was one of yours?"

"Yes."

"I was so scared when I realized I was being followed, Matteo," I confessed.

If I thought my words would soften him, they did the opposite. His eyes narrowed, and his voice became colder.

"You were lucky this time. I can't always be there to rescue you, Evie. It is tiresome. One of these times, I won't be able to help you." He crossed his arms. "I expected better of you."

His tone and anger cut me to the quick. I swallowed, unsure how to explain. I stepped forward, reaching for his arm, and he stepped back.

"Do not touch me."

I reared back as if he had slapped me.

"It was only the mall, Matteo."

His glare became icy. "Convenience store," he snapped.

"What?"

"Gianna went to the convenience store to get us a treat. She was walking home when they grabbed her. She was fourteen. Taken away because she was alone, beautiful, and no one was watching," he bit out, his voice frosty. "I will not allow that to happen again."

"I—I'm sorry," I whispered, hearing the anguish in his voice and understanding his fear more now.

"I have work I need to take care of. Your little joyride has cost me considerable time and expense. Neither of which I appreciated." He walked a wide path around me. "I'll be in my office until late. I'll see you tomorrow."

He walked out, leaving me reeling.

I spent the evening alone, and Matteo never came to our room all night. I assumed he slept in his office. I waited in the morning, hoping he would appear, and when he finally did, he looked as terrible as I felt. He walked in, holding the garment bag containing my dress and one with the shoes and laid it across the chair. Before he got to the bathroom, I spoke.

"Do I need those anymore?"

"Unless you don't want to accompany me to the dinner," he replied, not looking at me as he pulled off his clothes.

"Matteo, I'm sorry. For interrupting your work, making you come and get me. For worrying you."

He stalked closer. "I don't give a shit about my work or the interruption. What were you thinking, Evie? You broke the one promise I asked of you. How can I trust you?"

"I didn't set out to do that."

"Explain yourself."

I sighed. "I just wanted to pick out my own dress, Matteo. For months, I was told by Blaine what to wear, when to wear it, how to style my hair. Everything. I wanted to pick what I wore. Have a pedicure. That was all I planned." I wiped a hand over my weary eyes. "I knew you wouldn't be happy about Lila not being with us, but it felt silly not to go because of it."

"And then?"

"When Roza got the call, I truly meant to call Geo and go home. But then I discovered I had left my phone at home." I met his frosty glare. "I'm still not used to having one."

He pursed his lips but let me continue.

"Once my pedicure was done, I thought a little more time wouldn't matter. And then, frankly, I just forgot."

"You forgot," he repeated, sounding incredulous.

"Yes. I was picking things I liked. Enjoying being able to wander and look. Touch things. Try them on. I forgot everything but the simple womanly joy of shopping for something pretty. Picking up a gift for my husband." I shrugged. "As crazy as it sounds, I lost track of time."

Something strange passed over his face. His lips twisted, and he headed back to the bathroom.

"I hope it was worth it."

MATTEO

I drained my cup of coffee, reaching for the pot I'd had Marcus bring into the office for yet another cup. I glanced at my watch, seeing it was barely noon. It was going to be a long day. I stared at the papers in front of me, all the facts my team had been amassing on the current situation at my fingertips. I rubbed a hand over my eyes and brought my attention back into focus. I realized the room was silent, and I looked up, meeting the expectant faces of my men. They were obviously waiting for me to say something.

The anger that had been slowly simmering under my skin bubbled. "I missed that. Repeat yourself," I barked.

Damien, one of the younger crew, frowned. "I said it is going to be difficult to choose the right entry point. The security is so tight, if we choose the wrong one, everyone else will be alerted to our presence, and the mission will be blown."

"It's your job to make sure that doesn't happen," I snapped.

He grimaced. "Are you not listening, Matteo? Did you not read the report I gave you?" He flipped his hand in impatience. "Where the fuck are you today because you're certainly not with us on this."

The bubbling became a raging fire spreading its tendrils through my body.

"I beg your pardon?" I snapped.

"Enough, Damien," Marcus warned. "I think we should reconvene tomorrow."

"No," Damien sneered. "If any of us were this distracted, Matteo would have our balls. Or is that it, Matteo?" He focused on me. "Your new wife has your balls in such an uproar, you're no longer effective as our leader?"

I had to grip the edge of the table to stop myself from lunging at him. "What did you say?"

"You heard me. You pick up a piece of tail at the warehouse and, of all things, marry her, and now she leads you around by your cock. Maybe you need another trip to the mall with her. She—"

He never finished his thought. I had no recollection of moving, but suddenly, Damien was shoved against the wall, my hand pressing on his throat and my gun pointed to his head.

"That is my wife," I spat. "By disrespecting her, you are disrespecting me." I cocked the gun. "No one disrespects me and remains standing in this group."

His eyes were huge, no longer challenging, but pleading. I felt the slickness of his skin under my fingers and heard his labored breathing.

"Matteo," he choked out. "Please."

I pressed the gun harder, the metal sinking into his skin. "I protect my family. I don't give a fucking shit if you don't like it. You have a choice. Apologize and leave. Don't apologize and leave in a body bag."

"Matteo." Marcus's voice beseeched me at my elbow. "We need calm here. I'm certain Damien regrets his words."

"I-I do," he uttered, struggling for breath under my hold. "I was upset over the images—the heinous things I saw. I said things…" He trailed off. "I apologize."

Guilt flooded me, and I dropped my hand.

What the hell was I doing?

I stepped back, pulling away my gun, shocked at my behavior.

I put my hand on Damien's twitching shoulder. "I am the one who owes you an apology. I let my anger get the best of me."

"I shouldn't have said what I did," he replied. "I like Evie. We all like Evie. And I do respect you, Matteo. I was—" he swallowed "—I was upset, and I spoke out of turn."

Suddenly exhausted, I sat down, noticing we were the only ones in the room. Marcus had obviously cleared my office when I lost it. I remembered how it felt when I started this job. Seeing the horrors, unprepared for how they would affect me. I'd lashed out more than once, but Aldo had the patience to guide me through. I had failed Damien.

"Sit down," I said.

He hesitated, and I handed my gun to Marcus. "Sit," I repeated, indicating the chair.

"Let's talk."

Geo appeared in front of my desk a few hours later. He regarded me kindly, but he looked worried.

"You heard, I assume?" I asked.

"Are you all right?"

I blew out a long breath. "I will be." I ran my finger over the desk. "I was furious at Evie. Terrified when I found out she was out there alone. I took it out on Damien."

"Are you still mad?"

"I'm ashamed by my behavior."

"With Damien or Evie?"

"Both," I admitted. "I talked to Lila a little. She helped me understand Evie's side of things a bit more. I have to admit, I do not understand the draw of shopping, but she explained how easily Evie would have been carried away."

He smiled. "I don't understand it myself, but I know Lila can wander a mall for hours, come out with nothing, and still have had a wonderful time." He shrugged. "She likens it to me watching soccer. She doesn't get it, but she knows I can pass hours watching a ball get kicked around."

I appreciated his attempt at lightening the situation.

"I apologized to Damien. He is struggling, and I think I was able to help him—the way I should have in the first place."

"Instead of pulling your gun on him, you mean?"

"Yes."

"And Evie?"

"I said some things I am not proud of to her as well. I refused to listen."

He lifted a shoulder. "Typical behavior for a marital spat. You need to clear the air with her. You also need to forgive yourself, Matteo. You are only human after all."

"I thought I was ready to forgive her this morning, then when I saw her, I got angry again."

He stood. "Then work through your anger and talk to her. I am sure she is suffering as well." He smiled kindly. "You are new to this—all of this, Matteo. She brings out a side of you that you have never experienced before. She is trying to find her place in this life. There will be growing pains for both of you. But you will come back together and be stronger."

He left, his words repeating themselves in my head the rest of the day.

EVIE

I didn't see Matteo all day. Marcus came into the kitchen at lunch, and I handed him a plate of sandwiches.

"For anyone who wants them," I explained. "I'm sure Matteo is too busy being furious to eat." I paused. "I heard yelling. Angry yelling."

"There was…a situation. It's been handled."

"Is everyone all right?"

He nodded tersely. "Yes."

"Is he taking his bad mood out on the crew?" I guessed.

"He had a bad morning," was his reply. "He, ah, reacted. It happens."

"Really," I said sarcastically. "I hadn't realized."

"He'll calm down. Sometimes—sometimes, his anger gets the better of him, Evie."

"Good for him," I muttered.

I knew I had crossed a line, but Matteo refused to listen to me. One thing this incident had taught me was that I wasn't ready to be on my own in the world again. Recalling how terrified I had been when I thought I was being followed, I knew that now. When Matteo forgave me, he could at least find comfort in that fact. If he forgave me.

I got ready for the dinner, using the large closet to dress in. When I heard Matteo get in the shower, with a sad sigh, I slipped on the shoes and looked in the mirror. The dress was understated and pretty. The heels made me taller and showed off my legs. I looked different with my hair swept up and makeup on. The plain Evelyn I had always thought myself to be was gone, and Evie Campari was in her place.

Matteo entered the closet, clearly surprised to find me there. His eyes raked over me, the heat building in the room around us as he stared. Our eyes locked in the mirror, and I saw his reaction to me, the way his body tensed and his eyes became hooded. Then he broke our gaze and turned away.

"I'll be ready in ten minutes. Be at the front door," he commanded, reaching for a suit and striding from the closet, leaving me feeling devastated.

I wanted his praise. I craved his touch. I knew if he had seen me looking like this two days ago, we would have been late arriving to the dinner. My hair wouldn't have been perfect, and I would be covered in his scent.

Instead, I was empty and aching.

And, for the first time since that day in the warehouse, feeling utterly bereft.

Matteo was the perfect husband during the dinner. He introduced me, stayed close, and chatted with everyone at the table. He was constantly interrupted by people coming to see him, and he played his part very well. He was still intense, but it was tempered with humor. I understood why his business was so successful as I listened to him speak. He was extremely knowledgeable and well-thought-of. I was quiet for the most part, doing my best to act as if everything was fine and the man next to me was nothing but a loving new husband. He played the part well, accepting congratulations, introducing me as if he was proud. Though his hand hovered, it never touched. His gaze focused over my shoulder when he looked my way, bringing me into various conversations. More than once, he leaned over, looking to many as if he was bestowing a gentle caress to my skin or whispering in my ear. But his lips fell short of touching me, and the only words he uttered were instructions telling me to smile more, to stop playing with my clothing. On occasion, I was sure I saw a softening in his expression, a sadness flit over his face, but then he would blink, the expression disappearing.

I was grateful when the evening was over. The ride home was silent, the tension in the car so thick, you could cut it with a knife. At the house, as soon as we were inside, he strode away from me to his office. I stood alone in the hall, listening to the sound of the door closing, feeling more alone than ever.

Upstairs, I removed my makeup and hung up the dress I had been so excited to wear. The bags from my shopping expedition still sat on the floor, untouched, the desire to open them absent.

I washed my face and got into bed, already knowing Matteo would not join me. I lay for hours, unable to sleep, the pain in my chest twisting and burning.

I missed him.

I sat up as a thought hit me. Was he so angry he wouldn't be able to move past this? Had one bad decision on my part caused us irreparable damage? I knew he saw everything in black-and-white. But surely here, he could see the gray? I made a mistake. I had already paid for it, and I would never make it again. He had to know that. To believe me.

I was out of bed and headed down the steps quickly, my bare feet quiet on the carpeted floor. At his office, I hesitated, then pushed open the door, expecting to find him behind the desk. Instead, I found him on the sofa, bare-chested, his jacket and shirt flung over the back of the chair, his belt on the floor and his pants half undone, and one shoe off. There was a bottle of scotch open on the floor. He was asleep, his arm flung over his head. He didn't look peaceful, his mouth moving and frowning, muttering under his breath, his legs moving restlessly.

I kneeled beside him, the intensity of my feelings surprising me. His anxiety moved me, and without thinking, I laid my hand on his chest over his heart.

Instantly, his body relaxed. I lowered my eyes as his breathing changed, becoming deeper. I startled when I felt his arm move, and he covered my hand with his. Lifting my gaze, I met his intense stare. For a moment, there was silence. I opened my mouth, my voice pleading.

"Matteo, I'm sorry. *Please* forgive me. I can't–I can't—" I broke off with a sob, and suddenly he sat up, wrapping his arm around me and dragging me to his lap. He covered my mouth with his, kissing me with a fierceness that shocked and surprised me. He held me tight—so tight I could barely breathe—and he devoured me. His tongue was relentless, his body hard and unyielding against mine. I wrapped my arms around his neck, sliding my hands into his hair the way he liked, trying to understand what was happening. He fisted my nightgown, pulling it up my legs, and shifted as he yanked his pants down, his cock heavy and hot against my skin. He pulled my legs apart and buried himself inside me, his mouth never leaving mine. His thrusts were solid and powerful. Desperate and wanting. He growled and groaned deep in his throat. His grip on my hips was too tight, his mouth hard on mine. I clutched his shoulders, my nails scoring his skin, holding on as hard as I could. My body rose and fell with his, the passion between us sizzling and hot. The need overwhelming. Every stroke claimed, consumed, and possessed. Every pump of his hips screamed his anger, his worry, and his demand. Every slide of his tongue said what he couldn't.

Until the dam broke and he clutched me even tighter, burying his face into my neck as he climaxed, clenching me, shaking, and moaning my name into my skin. I trembled with the force of my orgasm, the swell of it powerful, making me whimper in a mixture of pleasure and pain as it tore through my body, leaving me gasping for air and exhausted.

We sat wrapped around each other, our bodies melded, still joined.

"Please forgive me," I whispered. "Please."

He sighed, his breath flowing over my skin.

"I have forgiven you, Evie. It's myself I can't forgive."

CHAPTER TWELVE

Matteo

I carried Evie upstairs, her warm body pressed to mine. I laid her back in our bed and slid in with her, turning to face her. In the dim light, her face was pale, the signs of her worry of the past couple of days evident.

I stroked her cheek.

"What do you mean, you can't forgive yourself?" she asked quietly. "I was in the wrong. I know that, Matteo. I went against your orders."

I sighed, thinking of how I had felt when I realized she had left the estate with only Roza. My first reaction hadn't been anger, but fear. Then when the situation was compounded by the fact that she hadn't called Geo, a strange sensation had occurred.

I thought she was running. She'd found a way out and was leaving me. The contemplation left me paralyzed. Devastated.

Marcus had leaned over. "Her phone is at the house, Matteo. I think she forgot it. She'd have no way of contacting Geo—or any of us, in fact."

The paralyzing fear left me when I realized he was right, and common sense took over. The anger bled back in. Not only had she left the house, she was now alone, with no way to contact anyone. A quick call to the salon confirmed what Marcus had guessed.

She had headed into the mall, and she was no doubt shopping.

"What is it that fascinates her so there?" I wondered out loud as the car sped toward the mall and I had called to have Neil head there and find her. "Stay back. Don't let her see you," I ordered. "But keep her safe."

Marcus shrugged, not meeting my eyes.

"What?" I snapped.

"She's a woman. Many of them enjoy shopping."

I waved off his words. When she appeared back at the salon, loaded down with bags but looking nervous and upset, I recalled them, but it didn't dissipate my fury.

I shifted, meeting Evie's anxious gaze.

"I was angry."

"I know. You wouldn't let me touch you."

"I was afraid if you did, I might hurt you, Evie."

Her eyes widened. "You would have struck me?"

"No." I paused. "I don't know. I doubt it, but I felt as if I was out of control. I wanted to punish you. I couldn't be around you." I cleared my throat. "In that moment, I was no better than the scum you had run away from."

She inched closer, her little body pressed to mine. She laid her hand on my cheek. "But you are. Don't you see, Matteo? You *didn't* hurt me. You walked away. You are a hundred times the man he ever was."

Then she swallowed. "But you not speaking to me hurt me more than the physical blow would have."

Her confession pierced my chest. Her words of assurance touched me. I held her close. "I'm sorry, *Piccolina*. It shook me. The whole thing." I paused. "When I first found out you were missing, I thought you'd left me."

"What?" She gasped. "Matteo, I told you I would never—"

I cut her off. "I know. The rational side of me understands that, but this new emotional side you have opened up is still growing, Evie. You have to understand. I am always in control. Always calm and rational. I have to be. I have to think on my feet, respond to any given situation with confidence. The second I heard you were out of the house and alone, I was frozen—ineffectual. And I responded to that by becoming angry."

"What changed?"

"Marcus reminded me I promised not to put you in a prison. Yet by denying you something as simple as a trip to the mall to pick out a new dress, I was doing just that. When you were out of the house, you did what you had been wanting to do and went shopping. Lila scolded me about my continued anger. I told her what you said about forgetting and she told me to think those words over, and I realized what she meant. You were having fun, and you forgot. You forgot about your past, about who you married. You were just a woman in a mall, without a man telling her what to do for a change. By denying you that, again, I was no better than him." I lifted her hand and kissed it.

"I did have fun," she confessed.

"I know. I saw you. You were so into the moment, looking at things, lost to everything else around you."

"You watched me?"

"I had to make sure you were okay. I only stayed a minute. You actually made me smile in spite of my anger," I admitted, recalling the moment.

"What was I doing?"

"Picking me new underwear, I think. Unless they were for Marcus. I haven't seen them yet, but you were certainly thorough in your inspection."

She slapped my chest. "Of course they are for you. Everything I bought is still in the bags."

I pressed her hand to my chest. "You were so beautiful at dinner. I loved your dress, the way you wore your hair. I was so proud to have you on my arm. You were elegant and graceful. Charming. A hundred times, I wanted to break down and ask for your forgiveness. But my pride stopped me." I met her gaze. "I'm asking now, Evie. Forgive me. Unpack your purchases and show me everything. Let me—let us—move forward."

"You are forgiven. I won't do it again."

"I think we both learned a lesson."

"Something else happened today," she said. "What was it?"

I told her about Damien. Not the exact words he said, just that he had been disrespectful and I had overreacted. She listened, not judging me.

"Because you were already angry at me," she said knowingly.

"I think so." I huffed a breath. "I find it hard to separate my feelings when it comes to you, Evie."

"Have you fixed things with Damien?"

"Yes. I spoke to Julian as well. Geo too. I'm ashamed of my behavior."

"You are only human. It happens to everyone."

"So people keep reminding me. I will do better."

"And I understand more now—about Gianna and your anxiety. I won't do it again," she promised. "When I thought I was being followed, all I could think about was getting back to you. You represent safety and home, Matteo. I was so scared that I wouldn't get back to you. I don't want to be a burden—"

Again, I cut her off. "I said that in anger. I didn't mean it. I'm sorry you were scared. I think we both need more time to adjust to our new life, yes?"

"Yes."

"The next time you want to shop, I'll send Neil with you. Marcus hates shopping unless it's for food. He trusts Neil, so therefore, I will as well. He has the patience of a saint and has no problem sitting in the mall while you wander to your heart's content. He has two teenage daughters, so he's used to it. You'll feel safe, and I'll know you're protected. Will that be acceptable to you?"

"You would be okay with that?"

"Not completely, but I'll learn. I don't want this place to be your prison, Evie, or you'll come to resent me. I love you too much for that to happen. I just need to know you're safe." I drew in a long breath. "To the world, you're simply my wife, Evie. To me, you are my world."

She gasped softly at my words. "I love you," she whispered.

"Am I really forgiven?"

"Yes, you are. Am I?"

"Yes." I kissed her. "Tomorrow, we start fresh, yes?"

"Yes."

EVIE

The next morning, Matteo had breakfast with me, smiling at me over his cup of coffee.

"What are your plans today?"

"I want to go visit Mrs. Armstrong in her new place."

"Fine. I'll send Marcus with you." He looked at me over his coffee cup. "Are you certain you don't want me to hire someone to oversee the place?"

Mrs. Armstrong would not be returning. She was recovering, but she could no longer work. Matteo had gotten her a lovely private room in a care home, and now that she had been transferred, I wanted to see her again.

"It was one thing when it was for a few weeks, but now it is permanent…" His voice trailed off.

"I'm sure. Maybe in a few months or, ah, when things change, but for now, I like looking after you and cooking. The rest is all done by the company she had hired. They have been doing it so long, both inside and out, it's like clockwork. They know exactly what to do, and it's no trouble."

"If you change your mind, you will tell me." It wasn't a question, but rather a statement.

"Yes."

"All right." He stood and bent over to kiss me. "I'm glad we're not fighting, although the make-up sex was fucking incredible," he growled low in my ear. "Both last night and this morning. I love it when you get all handsy and bossy with me, Mrs. Campari."

"Just a taste of your own medicine, Mr. Campari," I retorted. After last night's intense lovemaking, this morning, he had been sweet and loving, making me come with his mouth and taking me on our bed and again in the shower, his touches gentle, his body showing me we were okay once again.

His gaze softened, his mouth lifting at the corners. "Your medicine is far sweeter, my wife." He kissed me long and slow. "I'll see you tonight."

I watched him leave, feeling sad. I knew he struggled with what happened. With feeling less than perfect. He thought he had to be in control every moment of every day, but the bottom line was, that was simply not possible one hundred percent of the time. He regretted his anger and the feeling of being out of control. I knew, without a doubt, no matter how angry he was, he would never strike me. I didn't fear him that way, and he would figure that out. He would also find the balance between the man he had to be and the man he was. The boss when required, my husband the rest of the time.

I sighed wistfully. He had told me the next while would be busy for him. He had two situations he was working on, and he would be coming and going over the following few weeks. I already missed him. I couldn't think about the reason he'd be gone or what he would be doing. I still found that part of his life overwhelming and frightening. I didn't like that side of Matteo, although without it, I would probably be dead.

I shook my head to clear those thoughts and stood to get ready to go see Mrs. Armstrong.

———

The room Matteo arranged for Mrs. Armstrong was large and bright, with a lovely view of the gardens out back. She was in fine form, delighted with her new space. Matteo had all her personal things brought from the small apartment over the garage, and her room was homey and warm. She was pleased with the cookies and flowers I had brought her, and I went to the main kitchen and brought us tea. Marcus had a quick visit with her while I was out of the room, then headed to the waiting area so we could visit in private.

"Mr. Campari has been so generous," she told me as she sipped her tea. "I was so worried about having to live with my daughter and being a burden to her. Now, she can visit, I can go there whenever I want, and I have already made a couple of new friends. And there are so many activities to keep me busy," she enthused.

I patted her hand. "He appreciates all you have done, and he's happy to provide this for you. We both want you comfortable." Matteo could easily afford it, and I was pleased to know he had done this for her.

She beamed. "He is a good man. There aren't many men as busy and important as him who would come visit their old housekeeper or make sure they are so well looked after."

I smiled. "He is."

"I'm so glad he has you now. He needed his own angel." She shook her head. "He was alone too much."

I took a sip of tea, knowing Matteo would rather I not talk about him in too personal a fashion.

"How are you settling in? Finding everything all right?"

"Oh yes," I said. "The kitchen is lovely, and you had everything running so well, it isn't any trouble."

She nodded. "It took a while, but I found the right companies. The outside is the hardest. The turnover there is the largest, and you know Mr. Campari is very careful. They are very good about sending new employee information. He screens and approves them. Students and migrant workers are the hardest to retain."

"Of course," I murmured.

"The house staff has very few changes. I've had the same crew for over six years."

"The house is always immaculate," I agreed.

I changed the subject, and we talked about her daughter and grandkids for a bit. She shared a couple funny stories about Matteo, which made me laugh. When I saw she was getting tired, I stood. "I'll come back soon," I promised. I enjoyed talking to her.

"Oh, before you go, bring me my purse, please."

I handed it to her, and she reached in and withdrew a set of keys and a transponder. "My car and house keys and pass to get in the gate and open the garage door. I am sure Mr. Campari needs them back."

I took them, turning the transponder over, running my finger over the piece of tape.

"Oh," she whispered. "Don't tell them. I could never remember the password to get back in, so I wrote it on that piece of tape. Pull it off before you give it to him."

Recalling the Post-it note she had hidden under her old laptop, I held back my grin. "I will."

She sighed and closed her eyes. "Thank you for coming, dear."

"You're welcome."

I slipped the keys and transponder into my purse then went downstairs to Marcus.

When we pulled into the garage at the house, I showed him the transponder and the keys. He chuckled. "We all knew she couldn't remember. We put a new piece of tape on the back every time we changed her code. I'll just put it in the car. Matteo hasn't decided what to do with it."

"I could drive it."

He laughed. "When he decides you can drive on your own, Evie, the car he gets you will be much better than a little Toyota."

I rather liked the little Toyota, but I didn't argue. I needed to pick my battles.

For the next while, life seemed almost normal. As normal as life could be when you were married to a man like Matteo. I didn't question his time away, knowing he wouldn't discuss it. He kept that part of his life closed off. The house was quieter, feeling empty without him, even though the rooms at the other end of the house still held crew members who were constantly busy. I rarely ventured to that side, knowing Matteo preferred me not to. When he returned, he seemed fine, although I noticed he held me tighter and liked to find reasons to be around me. I was pleased to think I brought him some measure of peace.

The second time he went away, I decided I had been patient long enough. In the morning, I made a tray of muffins, brewed a pot of coffee, and let myself into the room used by Roza, Lila, and Gianna. I was early, and I sat at the empty desk beside the spot where I knew Gianna worked every day. When the door opened a short time later, I looked up to see her falter as she entered. Vince followed her, offering me one of his wide smiles. "Hey, Evie."

"Hello, Vince."

I had noticed Vince didn't always go with Matteo. Marcus was a constant and a few others, but Vince stayed behind, presumably due to Gianna. I found it touching he put his wife ahead of everything else.

Gianna crossed to her desk, tugging off her jacket. She wore a long-sleeved shirt and dark pants. Her hair was swept into a long ponytail. She was beautiful but looked upset as she sat down, her dark eyes, so much like Matteo's, regarding me nervously.

"Hello, Gianna."

She nodded. "Evie."

"I'll leave you ladies to it. Okay, Gianna?" Vince asked softly.

She hesitated, then sighed. "Yes."

"I'll be back later. Wait, are those muffins?"

I chuckled. "There's a basket of them in the kitchen."

He rubbed his hands together. "I'm off, then. See you later."

He closed the door, and for minutes, the room was silent. Finally, I couldn't take it anymore.

"How are you today, Gianna?"

"I–I'm good. How are you settling in?"

I huffed out a big breath. "I would be lying if I said it was all good. It's an adjustment."

"Is Matteo being difficult?"

The question surprised me. "No, it's an adjustment for him as well. He is trying to help me."

I lifted the coffeepot, pouring us each a cup, adding cream and sugar, and offering one to her. She accepted it with a smile. "You know how I like my coffee?"

"I asked Matteo." I picked up the muffins. "He said blueberry was your favorite."

She took one, biting it and closing her eyes. "These are so good. Thank you." She ate a few mouthfuls, then set the muffin on her desk.

"Evie, I know you're married to my brother, and I know I've not been welcoming. I'm sorry."

I shook my head. "I'm not here to make you feel bad, Gianna. I was hoping to get to know you a little more. Perhaps become friends. I miss Matteo when he is gone, and I'm lonely."

"I—I'm not very comfortable with new people."

"I know, and if you prefer that I go, I will. But you're my sister-in-law now, so I'd like to get to know you."

She studied me for a moment, then offered me a tremulous smile. "I can't believe Matteo got married."

I smiled in return. "I wasn't exactly on his radar, and he certainly wasn't on mine." I leaned forward, earnest. "I love him, Gianna. Somehow, it was meant to be. I thought my life was going to end that night, but he saved me. And I fell in love with him."

"And he with you. He talks about you all the time when he comes to see me."

"He does?"

"Yes." She sighed. "I know you know my story. I appreciate how patient you have been with me, but I would like to get to know you."

I couldn't hide my delight. "Really?"

"Yes." She bit her lip, then spoke again. "I know Matteo isn't an easy man to love. He became what he did because of me. I owe him everything."

"He doesn't regret his choices. He loves you very much."

"I know. He and Vince watch over me so well. I know I'm not in any danger. I have an extremely sheltered life, but that is my choice. I'm happy and content. Matteo has denied himself all these years. He's been missing something, and I think he finally discovered it when he found you. However you met, whatever the circumstances, you make my brother very happy, so I would like to try to get to know you." She smiled, looking shy. "You must be very special for Matteo to love you as he does."

She reached out and covered my hand. I noticed she shook slightly, but I patted her hand with mine. "Thank you, Gianna. It means a great deal to me, and I know it will to Matteo as well."

"Are you going to join us here?"

"I would like to—at least some of the time. I like looking after the house and Matteo."

"I'm glad. He needs that. I'll look forward to you being here more."

Lila and Roza walked in, shocked to see me.

"Evie!"

"Hi, Lila. Good morning, Roza. Gianna and I were having coffee. Would you like some?"

"Yes."

"Roza?"

"Please!"

Gianna lifted the basket. "She made muffins too. I was just going to tell her more about what it is we do here."

Lila met my eyes with a small smile. She accepted a muffin and sat next to me.

"Go ahead, Gianna. Tell Evie about our work. I think she'll fit in just fine."

Gianna hesitated, then nodded. "I think so too."

CHAPTER THIRTEEN

Evie

Life took on a different rhythm. I filled my days cooking, swimming, exploring my new home, and working on the little herb garden I had created. Two days a week, I spent with the other women, slowly learning what they did. The complex web of monies they handled. It was astronomical.

Evenings were always with Matteo when he was home. His time away increased, and I hated it every time he left—especially when one night stretched into two or more. I passed a lot of time in the library reading, as well as in the kitchen. It was a comfortable, homey room. Well laid out, the kitchen had another spot with an enormous wingback chair by the fireplace where I could read and a built-in desk I liked to sit at to write lists or use the tablet to look up recipes. For the first time in my life, I didn't have to work, and I enjoyed playing housewife. When he was home, Matteo came in for lunch. Often, he would hurry in a few times a day for coffee, to grab some cookies, and he never left without kissing me long and hard. A couple of times, he lifted me to the counter and took me. No one ever came into the kitchen while he was there, and I knew they never would. Matteo would never allow that to happen, so I was safe to enjoy his spontaneous amorous side. In the evening, he appeared by eight, and we ate dinner at the table. He opened a bottle of wine, loosened his collar, and became my Matteo. Warm, loving, and affectionate. Then we would retire to our room and spend the rest of the night exploring each other.

And then things changed.

After one lengthier time away, lunches ceased, and more times than not, the sandwiches I had Marcus take him came back uneaten. Matteo started coming to dinner later, some nights never showing up. At first, I went in search of him, but I encountered Vince outside the office every time, and he just shook his head.

"Not now, Evie."

Matteo came upstairs later and later, and often, I was asleep by the time he came to bed. He was usually gone when I woke up. The rare times he appeared before I fell asleep, he would shower, slide into bed, and without a word, take me, his touch needy and desperate. The only words he spoke were in passion, as he groaned and shook above me.

"I need you, my wife," he would whisper. "I love you, Evie."

But he no longer held me.

When I woke up this morning, I realized he hadn't touched me in almost a week. The last three nights, I'd slept alone.

In desperation, I talked to Lila, who listened quietly as I spoke.

"I feel as if I'm losing him somehow. I don't know what I've done wrong."

She sighed, rubbing my arm. "Nothing, Evie. Matteo is very new at this." She paused. "I shouldn't tell you this, but they are working on a new situation. Geo said it was horrendous, but that was all he would tell me. I think this is Matteo's way of trying to protect you. He becomes obsessed and *different* when a case is intense."

"Different?"

"Do you remember when you met him?"

"Yes." I shivered, thinking of that night. His coldness, and the fact that I had watched him kill people without blinking or showing remorse.

"I think," she began and sighed again. "I think he is finding it harder, given the more tender edge you have brought out in him. There are two sides to him, and he is trying to keep them separate."

"I know who I married. I accepted that when I agreed to become his wife."

"I know. And he will figure out the balance. Be patient and love him. He will come back to you, and once he does, you can talk to him about it."

"All right. I will try."

She glanced over my shoulder. "You have a lot going on over there."

"It's our two-month anniversary. I'm making Matteo his favorite dinner. I even made special cookies that Marcus delivered earlier to remind him. I hoped they would make him smile."

"I'm sure the date will not escape him." She stood. "I should get back. I'll see you soon."

"Yes."

She left, and I finished dinner preparations. I went upstairs, showered, and changed into one of Matteo's favorite dresses. Midnight blue, with an off-the-shoulder neckline that left my collarbone bare. He had informed me it was sexy the one time I wore it, and I wanted everything tonight to be what he liked.

I set the table with candles and flowers. At eight, I got the food ready.

Then I waited.

At eight-thirty, I knocked at his office door, but it never opened. I tried the handle, but it was locked.

At nine, I blew out the candles.

By nine-thirty, I put away the food, then, too tired and sad to worry about the rest of the kitchen, went to bed.

I poured a bath and slid in, still hoping Matteo would rush in full of apologies and we would make love in the tub. Then we could go downstairs and raid the refrigerator together as we had done a couple of other times, and the night would be salvaged.

But he never came.

I tried to read, but I couldn't concentrate. I curled into bed, wrapping my arms around his pillow, and gave in to tears.

I was still alone when I woke in the morning. I dragged myself from bed, got ready, and went to face the cleanup of the kitchen. However, I was surprised to find the kitchen cleaned. I wondered if perhaps Lila had done it, but at that point, it didn't matter. I began to look around, mentally preparing the day's menu, when I stopped.

Why was I bothering? Matteo wasn't going to show up for dinner tonight either. If our anniversary meant nothing to him, then why was I continuing to spend hours cooking, only to throw out the food?

I sat in the wingback chair, feeling dejected and confused. I stared out the window at the lush grounds. People were working away, keeping it beautiful and pristine.

Yet, no one ever used or enjoyed it. It was a waste.

It hit me.

Just like this house.

It wasn't a home. It was a façade for Matteo's task force. It was where they planned their missions, plotted the deaths of those whom they caught.

I shivered. Matteo had stated he wanted a family. Children. I glanced around, trying to imagine happy little toddlers in this large, rambling house. Would their laughter ring out, or would they be silenced, cast to an unused spot in the house so as not to disturb anyone?

Tears filled my eyes at the thought. I wouldn't allow that. I wanted my children raised in a home filled with light and love. For them to be happy. Was that possible here?

"I fear your clothing is suffering again."

I started at the sound of Matteo's voice. He stood a few feet away, his hands in his pockets. He looked exhausted, his shoulders bent and his expression weary.

I dashed away the tears from my cheeks and stood.

"I'm sorry, coffee is not yet made." I slid by him. "I'll send Marcus your mug once it is ready."

"Evie—"

I ignored him. "Did you want breakfast? After all, you missed dinner last night."

"Breakfast would be most appreciated."

I hated his formal tone. "Perhaps you could sleep once you've eaten," I informed him, trying desperately not to fling my arms around him and beg him to talk to me. To let me in.

"I slept on the sofa in my office."

Those words hit me, making my chest ache.

"Your sofa must be more comfortable than our bed since you spend more time sleeping there than you do with me these days."

"I didn't wish to disturb you."

I rolled my eyes at that weak excuse, huffing a sigh as I took a mug from the cupboard. "Whatever," I muttered.

"I don't like that frown on your face or that rude expression," he snapped.

I slammed the mug I was holding on the counter, my anger taking over. "And I don't like being ignored! Where were you last night, Matteo? You missed our anniversary dinner. In fact, where are you any night these days? At least you tried when we first got married!"

He crossed his arms. "I'm a busy man. Something I explained to you when we got married."

I glared. "You also promised me respect. There is nothing respectful about the way you are treating me."

He narrowed his eyes. "Careful, Evie," he warned lowly.

"Or what?" I challenged. "You'll hit me? We've already established I'd prefer that to your indifference."

He remained silent, regarding me intently.

I was too mad to care. "You said you loved me, and I was your entire world. You told me if I needed you, I only had to ask. But last night, you ignored my knock and left me alone on a date that meant a great deal to me. Do you know how that made me feel? Cast aside yet again?"

"It is something you will have to get used to. Deal with it, Evie. And stop hiding in the kitchen. Go work with the girls more and do something useful."

I shook my head. "Is there no satisfying you, Matteo? I'm not *hiding*. I still make your sister uncomfortable, and I'm trying to give her time to get used to me. I thought I was doing something useful," I added, a catch in my voice.

"And what would that be?"

"Trying to look after my husband. That, to me, was important. I'm sorry you felt I was wasting my time." I turned away to hide my fresh tears. I reached for the toast that had popped up, the edge burning my finger. I dropped it with a low exclamation, shaking the smarting digit. Matteo appeared beside me, grabbed my hand, and inspected the small blister.

"It's fine," I insisted, pulling my hand away. "Leave it."

With a low growl, he picked up my hand, checking it out. He lowered his head, kissing the end of my finger, then slid it into his mouth, easing the burn with the cool swipe of his tongue. His eyes met mine, blazing with intensity. I couldn't look away.

"I'm sorry," I whispered.

Slowly, he pulled my finger from his mouth, kissing the end. "Your anger is justified, Evie. I understand it. Your frustrations drive it. My fear drives mine."

He wrapped my hand in his. "I'm not doing a good job being a proper husband to you," he confessed in a low tone.

I seized the opportunity to get him to open up to me.

"Lila says you have a terrible assignment."

"Yes. It is very…difficult." He huffed out a deep breath. "Sometimes, the images are burned into my brain, and I can't see anything else, Evie. I don't want to poison our marital bed by bringing those images with me."

My anger dissipated, seeing the pain in his eyes and hearing the torment in his voice.

"Maybe if you'd let me hold you and lose yourself with me, I could help erase those images." I dared to reach up and cup his cheek, running my fingers along his tense jaw. "At least for a short while."

He furrowed his brow.

"I want to help you, Matteo. I want to be a good and supportive wife to you, but you have to allow me to do so."

Suddenly, I was in his arms, encased fully in his embrace, with his mouth hard on mine. His kiss was desperate and possessive. His body screamed of tension and need. He held me tight, crushing me so close I could barely breathe. His hands never stopped in their exploration, tugging at my clothes and dipping underneath to find my skin that longed for his touch. I whimpered as he lifted me to the counter, and he licked and nipped at my neck, his groans muffled and low.

"I need you *now*. Right fucking now." He buried his hands in my hair, forcing me to look at him.

"Don't deny me this. Tell me yes. *Please* forgive me and tell me yes."

"Yes," I whispered.

Seconds later, he slammed into me. There was nothing gentle or sweet. It was possession and claiming. His need was rampant. He gripped me, his thrusts deep and steady, his breath hot on my neck.

"Evie, oh God, *Piccolina*. You…*I need*…fuck!"

I cried out his name, letting him take me, needing him as much as he needed me. I began to tighten around him, moaning and pleading, wanting to feel him as deep as he could be. He lifted my legs, shoving them against my chest, and pushed harder. Deeper. Hitting a spot I didn't know existed.

Seconds later, I came. Hard, shaking, and crying out his name. He followed soon after, collapsing on my chest, panting and sweating. His face was buried in my neck, and I was startled to feel the dampness of his tears on my skin. Wrapping my arms around him, I kept him close, running my fingers through his hair in soothing caresses.

"I'm here, Matteo. For you. You need to let me in."

He tightened his arms, then drew back and allowed me to see his torment.

"This case is horrendous. It's killing me," he confessed. "The images and atrocities are beyond even my comprehension. It leaves me so ill, I'm having trouble coping."

I ran my fingers through his hair. "Don't shut me out, Matteo. Come to me. Let me be the light for you."

"I come to you each night, Evie."

"But I wake up alone," I said, confused.

"I cannot bear to wake you. I worry I will disturb you since I cannot sleep. I watch over you as you slumber. It gives me the only peace I find these days." He frowned. "Except the past few nights, you haven't been resting. You're fitful, and you cry out in your sleep. You calm when I hold your hand, but you still seem to need something."

I cupped his face. "I need you, Matteo. I sleep well in your arms. Without them, without *you*, I am lost now."

His eyes widened. "But I…"

I shook my head. "Even if you can't sleep, even if you need to make love to me or talk to me all night, I would prefer that to an empty bed and not feeling as if I am enough for you."

He crushed me to him. "You are, my beauty. You are all that keeps me going right now."

"Then show me."

"I don't know how." He shrugged his shoulders. "This is so new to me. I don't know how to let you help me."

"Where is everyone?"

"They are all exhausted. We're waiting for some more information before we proceed. I sent them home until lunchtime to rest."

"Then come upstairs with me and sleep. I'll hold you, and you can rest."

He hesitated.

"Please, Matteo. For me."

Without another word, he lifted me into his arms and carried me upstairs.

For the first time in days, I felt complete.

CHAPTER FOURTEEN

Evie

Matteo slept hard. With his body curved around me and his face buried in my neck, he was out instantly. I ran my fingers through his messy hair and watched him. Even in sleep, he appeared distressed, his brow furrowed and his full lips pulled into a frown. Gently, I traced the dark circles under his eyes, hating the exhaustion written on his skin.

He burrowed closer. "Need you," he mumbled. "Love you so much…"

I vowed not to let him push me away again. He needed me. He loved me. I wouldn't let him down.

Later, when he woke and showered, I made him a late breakfast, tsking as he wolfed it down. He was starving.

"I missed your cooking," he admitted.

"You need to eat. No more skipping meals and not coming to our bed. No matter how awful the day is,

Matteo. Your men need you to be strong, and ignoring your health is not helping." Leaning over, I cupped his cheek. "I need you."

He covered my hand with his own. "I need you, as well." He sighed. "I will try to do better, Evie."

"I know you will."

He reached into his pocket and pulled out a small box, setting it on the table.

"What is that?"

"Your anniversary present."

Tears filled my eyes. "You did remember?"

"Yes. I had planned to be here, celebrating with you. Then Julian called, and everything went to hell." He drew in a long breath. "I was so sickened by what I found out that I couldn't face you. Anyone. I coped the only way I knew how."

"By being alone."

"Yes."

"No more, Matteo. Even if you are struggling— especially if you are—you need to come to me. If you can't talk, it's fine. Just let me be there for you."

He studied me for a moment, then captured my hand, pressing his lips to my palm. "I will."

He nudged the box my way. "I had this made for you. I hope you like it."

I opened the lid, my eyes widening at the sight. A pretty necklace, delicate and lovely, was nestled on the velvet. It contained a tiny polished stone, a piece of a shell, and a creamy white pearl, arranged in a clear locket. All things I had found on our honeymoon and brought home. The pearl had been in the oysters we ate one night. The stone had glittered in the water, and I had never seen colors like the broken shell had possessed. Matteo had teased me about the silly items but never mentioned them after we got home—I assumed he had forgotten about them. They had sat in a small cup on the shelf, and I had planned to do something with them, but he had this made for me instead.

"It's a reminder for you of our honeymoon. I had the stone polished, so it looks the way it did in the water, and the jeweler smoothed out the edges of the shell." He stood and fastened the delicate chain around my neck, pressing a kiss to the nape, then sat back down. "You can think of happier times when you wear it."

"It's perfect. Thank you." I touched the cool metal. "I didn't get you anything. I wanted to make you your favorite dinner."

"May I have a do-over?"

"Yes. Tonight?"

He shook his head, looking regretful. "Saturday. I promise you, Saturday night and Sunday, you have me."

"All right. I can live with that."

He drained his mug and stood. "I'll see you later then, my wife." He kissed me, his mouth lingering. "Thank you."

I watched him walk away, his shoulders held back and broad. Although still tense, he wasn't as beaten down. He was strong and sure.

I was determined to make sure he remained that way.

He liked it when I did things he didn't expect. He'd been thrilled when he found out I had made the effort to reach out to Gianna. He loved it when I initiated our lovemaking. He'd even admitted he liked my anger.

"It is rare anyone talks back to me," he'd admitted. "For my tiny slip of a wife to challenge me——" he grinned "——frankly, it turns me on."

I stood, a plan forming. I had no doubt, even if he had good intentions, as soon as he was back behind his desk, he would forget about what I had said. Forget about eating or looking after himself. Forget I was here and wanting to help him.

I decided I wouldn't allow him to forget.

Around nine o'clock, I walked down the hall, carrying a tray. I had sent a sandwich with Marcus earlier in the day, and the plate had been returned empty, so I knew Matteo had eaten. But a sandwich wasn't enough to keep him going. I took a deep breath as I approached the door, which stood ajar. I heard voices, papers rustling, keyboards being used, and I paused, waiting until I could pick out the timbre of Matteo's voice.

"We have everything we need now. We need to move quickly before he slips through our fingers again. He is getting more out of control."

"Which gave us our break." I heard Vince speak.

"Yes," Matteo replied. "We move in three days. Everything will be in place. We end this—and him." He paused. "I look forward to extinguishing all of it."

There were murmured approvals as I shivered at the tone of his voice. But this was the right time for me to interrupt.

I raised my hand and knocked loudly. The door flung open, and Marcus looked at me, startled. "Evie? Is there a problem?"

"Yes." Hiding my nerves, I walked into the office, knowing half a dozen pairs of eyes were on me, none more intense and curious than my husband's.

"Gentlemen, in the kitchen, you will find a pot of stew and freshly baked bread. The table is set, and you can help yourself to food."

No one moved.

I cleared my throat. "I have dinner for my husband, and I must insist he eat. That you *all* eat. You need your strength."

All eyes went to Matteo. He stared at me, one finger running over his bottom lip, reminding me of the night he had found me. He stood unhurriedly, unfurling his body from his chair.

"My wife's cooking is not to be missed. Go and eat. I will let you know when you can return."

They nodded and left, their quiet thanks a hum in the air. Marcus was the last one out, shutting the door behind him.

Knowing Matteo wanted me shielded, I chose a sofa in the corner of his large office, away from the computers and files scattered around. I sat down, setting the tray on the table. "I have your dinner. Please eat."

He sat beside me, and I handed him the steaming bowl. He settled back, draping a napkin over his lap. I tried not to gawk at how incredibly sexy he looked, but it was impossible not to notice. He had his shirt sleeves rolled up, showing his toned forearms, the tie loosened with the top two buttons of his shirt undone. His hair was a mess, meaning he had run his fingers through it repeatedly. He met my gaze, smirking at me.

"Like what you see, my wife?"

"Very much."

His smile returned, letting me know he was pleased.

He tried a mouthful, chewing slowly, savoring the taste. I picked up my smaller bowl, tucking my leg under me and taking a mouthful. Matteo didn't speak for a while, but he hadn't thrown me out either. He ate steadily for a few minutes, then cleared his throat.

"This is delicious."

"Thank you."

"Unexpected, but delicious."

I lifted my gaze, meeting his eyes. I wasn't sure how he would react to my unanticipated move, but I was pleased to see a teasing glint in his stare. I knew he had to be hungry and tired by now.

"How bold you're being this evening, Mrs. Campari. Checking me out, plying me with food. Braving the lion in his den, so to speak."

I lifted one shoulder, not saying anything.

He chewed another mouthful, wiping his lips with his napkin. "Walking into my office, telling my men to go eat dinner that you prepared for them. Without even asking my permission to speak to them. Then demanding I eat. Very brazen of you." He quirked his eyebrow, letting me know he was in no way angry. "Very shocking."

"You're my husband. It is my job to look after you. No matter how hard you resist."

He shook his head. "I have no desire to resist." He leaned forward, pressing his lips to mine. "I am, in fact, delighted by your show of bravery."

"Oh?"

He kissed me again, this time with more force. "I am rather turned on by this side of you, my Evie."

"*Oh*," I repeated.

He glanced at the tray. "Did you bring dessert?"

"No. The tray was too full."

He pursed his lips and nodded sagely. "Well then, I suppose I will have to improvise." His eyes darkened as he studied me. "Eat your dinner. You'll need your energy for what I have in mind for after."

"After?" I whispered, suddenly no longer hungry.

"I have a craving for dessert. One only you can ease."

"Your team?" I breathed out, desire coursing through me at his veiled words.

"Will not return until I tell them to." He leaned forward, pressing his lips to my throat. "I believe I will let them enjoy a long"—*kiss*—"leisurely"—*kiss*—"meal."

He sat back, a wicked grin on his face. "I know I intend to."

I began to place my bowl on the table, but he stopped me with a smile. "Eat. Trust me, you'll need it."

He rose and went to a bar in the corner. He poured some brandy into a snifter and walked toward me, swirling the contents in the glass as he watched me. I finished my bowl, setting it on the table. Silently, he offered me the tumbler, and I sipped the decadent liquor, then handed him back the glass. He drank the rest and sank to his knees in front of me. He tugged on his tie, pulling it over his head.

"I think we should try something different."

My heartbeat skyrocketed. "Okay."

"Do you trust me?"

I didn't hesitate. "Yes."

"Close your eyes."

I did as he requested, then felt him slip his tie over my eyes, tightening the silky fabric to my head. He pressed his mouth to mine. "How you please me, Evie," he murmured against my lips.

I whimpered as he slipped his fingers down the front of my blouse, unhurriedly unbuttoning the fabric. "I love undressing you. It's like unwrapping a precious gift." He tugged it open, tracing the lace of my camisole with his finger and making me shiver. "I never know what I will find."

He had confessed his love of lingerie while we were on our honeymoon. When we returned, I had spent a small fortune on wispy scraps of lace he loved to pull from my body. I had already replaced several pieces. Tonight, though, he tugged down the cups, pushing my breasts over the top. Locked in darkness, I cried out softly when his lips closed over my nipple, tugging hard.

"I love how responsive you are."

He hooked his fingers into my waistband and removed my pants and lacy thong in one swift move. He clasped his hands on the tops of my thighs, spreading me wide. I whimpered as his hot breath drifted across my aching center.

"Dessert," he murmured. "Evie-flavored honey dripping down my throat. My favorite."

I moaned as his mouth covered my clit, sucking gently. He played and teased with his tongue, and my hand flew to his head, holding him close, the pleasure intense.

He slid his hands under my ass cheeks, pulling me up and close, flinging my legs over his shoulders. He buried his face between my thighs and began fucking me with his mouth. He used his tongue and teeth to tease and suck. Nip and lick. He slid his fingers inside, thrusting them deeply, taking me to the edge fast. Unable to see, all I could do was feel. How warm his mouth felt on me, how his tongue slid against my sensitive core, the way his fingers curled inside me. He growled low in his throat, the vibration adding another sensation to my already overloaded nerves. He slipped his thumb into my ass, making me gasp and keen even more at the unexpected penetration.

I exploded, clamping my hand over my mouth to stifle my screams. Before I had a chance to recover, Matteo yanked me forward and buried himself inside me. It sent me back over the edge, and in only a few strokes, he followed. His ragged breaths were loud in my ear.

"What you do to me, Evie. Only you."

I stroked the back of his neck. "Good."

He pulled his tie off my eyes, and blinking, I met his gaze. The darkness that had lurked earlier was gone, and he looked relaxed.

"You have no idea how much I needed that. Needed you."

I smiled shyly. "Glad I helped."

"I think I'll send my men home. We can reconvene in the morning."

"You don't have to—"

He silenced me with his mouth. "But I do. I'm not finished with you yet. Not by a long shot. I'm taking you upstairs."

"Well then, by all means, send them home."

We separated and dressed, exchanging grins and long glances.

He picked up the tray. "You go and run a bath. I'll dismiss them and be up to join you shortly."

"The kitchen…"

"I assure you, once they tasted your stew, they devoured everything you had made, and knowing Marcus, the kitchen has been tidied." He looked at his watch with a chuckle. "It wouldn't surprise me if I found they were already gone."

"They would do that?"

He caressed my cheek. "Evie, we're men. I have never taken a supper break. The first time I ever took a lunch break was because of you. I think, given the length of time I've had the door shut, they figured it out, and Marcus would have told them to leave."

My cheeks flushed, and Matteo smirked.

"Don't be embarrassed. Hold your head up and show them who you are." He lifted my hand to his lips. "My everything, my brave wife."

I contemplated his words, then swept past him and up the stairs. His low laughter followed me until I rounded the corner on the top landing, then I began to giggle.

I hurried to our room and began to prepare the bath, already anticipating his arrival.

CHAPTER FIFTEEN

Evie

Matteo glanced at me over his cup of coffee, his gaze indulgent. He looked rested, despite keeping me up late. Some of the tension had disappeared around his eyes, although I knew it would build again.

"I thought I would go see Mrs. Armstrong this afternoon and do some grocery shopping."

A slight frown creased his forehead. "Can you do it next week?"

"You mean after you get home?"

His frown grew.

"I heard you last night, Matteo. I know you're going away." I drew in a deep breath. "When you come back this awful case that is upsetting you so much will be over."

For a moment, he said nothing then he nodded. "The final pieces have fallen into place, and we're ready to move." He passed a hand over his head. "He's been on my radar for a while, but he is good at escaping and hiding."

"Is it terrible?" I asked.

He took my hand. "It's the worst thing I've ever seen, Evie. Don't ask me for details—I can't share those with you. This man is a narcissist, a sociopath, and a psychopath rolled into one. I have never seen anything like it. I'm not sure I would even call him human."

I shivered at his words. "Then you need to do this."

"Yes. He needs to be wiped from the face of this earth. Him and every part of his organization."

I nodded. "How long will you be gone?"

"Two or three days." He looked at our clasped hands. "I need you to stay home while I'm gone, Evie. Since Vince, Marcus, and Alex are coming with me, Roza will stay here in the main house with Gianna. Geo and Lila will also."

"All right."

He nodded. "Go see Mrs. Armstrong and do your shopping. But then come home immediately."

I didn't argue. "I will."

"When this is done, Evie, I want to go away again. Just get away from all this…" He paused. "Violence."

"Back to your island?"

"Our island," he corrected gently. "What is mine is yours now. And yes, there, or if there's somewhere else you'd like to go, I would take you there."

"Matteo, I want to be wherever you are."

He regarded me in silence. "I often wondered what it would be like to have peace. You bring me that peace, Evie. In your presence, I find that. It is a gift I cannot fully explain."

His words brought tears to my eyes.

"There is no justice to be sought," he continued. "No blood shed. No pain or vengeance to extract." He sighed. "For the first time since I made my decision to join this fight, I see the end."

"What do you see at the end?" I asked.

He played with my fingers. "I see us. Living a quiet life somewhere, leaving all this behind." He frowned. "Would you like that?"

"Yes."

He stood. "Good. Now do your errands and come home to me."

He strode from the kitchen, and I finished my coffee. His reflections had shown me a future different from what I had feared. Different from what I pictured.

A future I hoped would come true soon.

I relaxed in the tub, the steam swirling around me. The sound of our bedroom door opening made me sit up. Matteo's tired face appeared around the door.

"Room in there for one more?"

"Always."

He came in, shrugging off his shirt. He undid his belt, allowing his pants to drop to the floor, leaving him in only his boxers. I watched as he tugged them down his thighs and stepped away from the pile of clothes. He stopped to pull his watch from his wrist and caught me studying him in the mirror.

"I like it when you watch me."

I slid forward, making room for him. I smiled as he walked toward the tub.

"I like watching you. You're very sexy."

He slid in, wrapping his arms around me, bringing me tight to his chest. He dropped his face to my neck.

"So brazen you are these days."

I giggled as he teased my skin with his tongue.

With a sigh, he leaned back, taking me with him.

"I have longed to be close to you all day, Evie."

I traced his hands, toying with his ring. "Are you all right, Matteo?"

"I will be."

I knew what he was telling me without words. Tomorrow was the day they were moving against their latest target. I knew what he had told me and how deeply this was affecting him, and he was very worried about it. He didn't like to talk about what he did, and I had been surprised he shared that much.

"I hate to see you go."

"I dread it," he stated honestly, then tightened his arms around me. "Evie, you must promise to stay here while I'm gone. There will be security and you will be safe, but I must have your word you will not leave."

I heard the tension in his voice. Felt his anxiety. "I know, Matteo. I made sure I had everything we would need. I won't leave, I promise."

He pressed a kiss to my head. "Thank you."

"I need your promise as well."

"Oh? What promise might that be?"

I turned and met his dark gaze.

"That you will come home safe to me, Matteo. I need you. I love you."

His eyes softened, and he cupped my cheek. "I will, Evie. We are ready, and once we shut down these lowlifes, I will come home to you. I will be back as fast as I can."

"I know."

"I have never had someone to return to until now. Until you."

"I will always be here."

He kissed me, his mouth hard and possessive. After a few moments, he rose, lifting me with him. He stepped out of the tub, water cascading off our skin, hitting the floor like raindrops. He laid me on our bed, hovering over me.

"I love you," he murmured.

I reached for him, pulling him down to me, needing to feel his weight on me. Needing to feel him.

"I love you, Matteo."

The house seemed bigger with Matteo gone.

He left in the middle of the night, his kiss hard and pressing on my mouth.

"Be safe," he ordered against my lips. "Do not leave this house. Promise me."

"I promise."

"I will be home as soon as I can."

"I'll be here."

He wrapped me in his arms, holding me close. "That is what I need to get through this."

Then he was gone.

I'd tried to fall asleep after he left, but the bed felt wrong without him, the house too silent. I got up and switched on a light. On my bedside table was a small box, and inside, a bracelet, beautiful and shimmering under the light. Our initials entwined, *M & E*, inlaid with tiny diamonds. A card inside the box simply read:

I want to see this on your wrist when I return.
We are linked, no matter the distance.
Yours always,
M

There were tears in my eyes as I examined the delicate piece. I slipped it on, fumbling with the clasp, but I finally got it locked. I crossed the room to place the box on the dresser, stopping as I saw Matteo's cell phone, wallet, and wedding ring on the wooden surface. I picked up the wide platinum band, sliding it on my finger. Matteo had long, elegant hands and fingers, but it was still loose on me.

I had bought it on one of my shopping trips and given it to him. I recalled the look on his face when he opened it, running his finger over the smooth band.

"You'd like me to wear a ring, Piccolina?" he asked.

"I notice you look at mine often. I thought perhaps you'd like one as well."

He slid it on his finger, making a fist and looking at it. "I like it." He looked up, smiling. "Marking me as taken, my wife?"

"Yes."

His smile had been wide with delight. "I will wear it with pride."

He had explained he took nothing personal with him, nothing that could tie him back to his world. He had assured me, in dire circumstances, should anything happen to him, I would be informed and taken care of. I understood his reasons and the need for the action.

Still, it shook me to see his personal things left behind every time he went away. For some reason, seeing them this time seemed more significant. With a sigh, I placed his ring on top of his wallet and got dressed. I knew I wouldn't be sleeping anymore tonight.

Hours later, Lila, Gianna, and Roza arrived together with Geo. He smiled and accepted a cup of coffee and a muffin.

"There are guards on the grounds and two inside. They will be discreet, but if you need them, you only have to call. I'll be back around six."

"You'll be here until Matteo returns?" I asked, my nerves getting the better of me.

He smiled kindly. "Yes, we all will be." He covered my hand with a gentle squeeze. "Be at ease, Evie. Matteo and his team are professionals. They are cautious, have backup plans, and will be covered. He will come home safe to you."

"Thank you, Geo."

"I'm only working today, then I'm off until they are back. Perhaps we can find something to entertain us this evening. Matteo has a large movie collection. Maybe a comedy?"

"That sounds good."

We stayed busy all day, all of us on edge. Gianna looked especially stressed, so I sat beside her, asking her to explain in more detail how they used the monies to help women and children. She was glad for the distraction, and she explained how they managed the large portfolio. I was still shocked when I saw the vast amount of money they handled.

"Roza is a savvy investor. Lila heads up the charity aspect, and I look after the individual requests." She offered me a shy smile. "Maybe you would like to work with me?"

"Yes, definitely," I said. "What do you do exactly?"

She pulled a file close. "Some of the people Matteo and his team rescue have no place to go or no family. We help set them up. A new identity, a home, anything they need." She sighed. "Some, like me, can never get over what happened to them, so we make sure they are set for life."

"How?" I asked. "That would be enormous to track."

"We own a dozen large properties all over the world. We let people live there, have a new life. Sort of like small communities, really. We have staff that run them. There are gardens they work in, farms, vineyards—a variety of places, all legal. They are employed, safe, happy, and looked after. That's what we strive to do."

"You use bad money to do something worthwhile."

"Yes."

I nodded. "I'm in."

Four days passed. I missed Matteo terribly. The sound of his voice. His touch. The way it felt to wake beside him. He was always so warm, and I felt safe with him close. I knew Gianna and Roza missed Vince and Alex as well. We kept one another's spirits up in the daytime, but once I headed to bed, I felt the sadness creep in.

I was also worried. Matteo had thought he would be gone two days, maybe three. Although Geo assured me this happened on occasion, I noticed even he seemed tense.

I couldn't sleep. At night, I paced our room, wearing one of Matteo's shirts. I jumped at every noise. I couldn't concentrate during the day. One night, I went downstairs and slipped into Matteo's office. It was deserted and silent. I sat behind his desk, pulling my legs up to my chest. There in this chair, I could smell his rich scent. It was soaked into the leather. His desk was in perfect order—he always left it that way, and no one used it while he was gone. Curious, I opened the top drawer, smiling when I saw a picture of me he kept there. He had obviously taken it on our honeymoon. I was sitting on the sand, my face lifted to the sun with a smile on my lips. The edges were worn as if he picked it up a lot, and it made my chest warm with the knowledge of how much I meant to him. I also discovered a stash of chocolate, and I shook my head. His sweet tooth must be even stronger than I knew. The picture I was holding dropped from my fingers, and I bent to pick it up, glancing at the underside of his desk. A gun was fastened to the wood on the bottom of the drawer, not visible to anyone, but easily accessed if needed. Right behind the drawer was another gun— smaller and even more concealed. I swallowed, suddenly fearful once again. It shouldn't surprise me Matteo had a gun at his desk. Even two. For all I knew, there were guns hidden in various places all over the house.

He always said I was safe here. There were men outside. Gates. Guns in the house. I wasn't sure if it made me feel safer—or more anxious.

I sat back in the chair, trying to battle down my nerves, one question burning in my mind.

Why wasn't Matteo home yet?

Geo's voice broke through my panic. "Evie."

I looked up, startled.

"Are you all right? It's three o'clock."

"I can't sleep. I'm worried."

He came in and crouched in front of me. "He will be home soon, Evie."

A tear ran down my cheek, but I nodded, trying to smile.

"This happens on occasion. They have to adjust, go to Plan B. All will be well."

"Do you ever get used to it?"

He shook his head. "No." He sat on the edge of the desk. "Matteo's father was my half brother. We were never close. After he died and Matteo went to live with Aldo, Vince's uncle, we became closer. When he decided to join this fight, I did as well in my own way." He lifted his shoulders. "As a physician, I can offer services that would have questions asked at a hospital. I am completely legal and my practice busy, but Matteo and

his crew come first. What he does—what his crew does
—is not something I'm involved in. And luckily, they are
careful, and my services are not required often. I have to
trust in Matteo, but like you, I worry."

"I saw a few scars," I whispered.

"Yes, they have all been hurt, but they are careful.
Matteo takes the lives and welfare of his crew very
seriously. And his own as well. Especially now." He
squeezed my hands. "I'm so pleased he has found you."

"I love him."

He stood and pressed a kiss to my forehead. "I know,
Evie. I know." He smiled. "I will leave you in peace. But
try to get some sleep. Matteo won't be happy when he
returns and you look tired."

"I'll try."

He left and I sat there, my head filled with questions and
my heart heavy. The one person I could talk to, could
ask, was out somewhere doing something I couldn't even
comprehend. At times, it was hard to reconcile the man
I first saw with the man I loved. I knew they were one
and the same, yet at times the dichotomy between them
was so great, it was hard to believe.

One a cold, ruthless killer with no qualms about taking a
human life. Exacting justice for those the criminals had
hurt—determined to save others from the fate his sister
had faced and punish those responsible.

The other, a tender, passionate husband who would do anything to protect me—even from himself. A man who had buried his emotions so deep, he forgot to live and was slowly learning to open himself back up to that side of life. Who so desperately craved the light he had turned away from.

That was my husband. Black-and-white. Dark-and-light.

Regardless of what happened outside this house, of right or wrong, he was mine and I loved him.

I curled up in his chair, surrounded by his scent.

CHAPTER SIXTEEN

Evie

The next day, I baked hundreds of cookies, my nerves so tight I couldn't sit down. Back and forth I went between the oven and the window, hoping somehow to see a car with Matteo in it coming through the gates.

The house smelled of cinnamon and spices, chocolate and sugar. I wanted to spoil Matteo when he got home.

He just had to get here.

Geo entered the kitchen, looking serious. My heart rate sped up.

"Geo, what is it?"

He held up his hand. "All is well. I had a message from Vince. They were delayed but will be home soon."

I sat down, my legs too shaky to hold me up any longer. "Okay. Th–That's good."

He crouched in front of me. "There are some injuries, Evie."

I felt myself go pale. "Matteo?"

"He is one of the ones hurt, yes. Not life-threatening, but I will check them out as soon as they get here."

"When will they be here?"

"Within two hours."

I stood. "All right. We need to be ready."

He smiled. "Yes."

A short while later, I was in the kitchen making coffee when I heard the front door open and slam into the wall. There was the sound of running feet, and Matteo's voice rang out in the quiet house.

"Evie!"

Footsteps pounded on the steps, and I hurried into the hall. "Matteo?"

He stopped, spinning on the staircase. He stared at me, then took the steps back down two at a time and yanked me into his arms. He was shaking and tense. He crushed me tight to his chest, lifting me off the floor.

"Oh, Evie. Evie," he whispered. *"Evie."*

He was terrifying me. "Matteo," I pleaded, running my hands over him. "I'm here."

He said nothing, and I pulled back, cupping his face. It was bruised, a cut over his eye that ran along his hairline, dried blood mixed with fresh on his skin. His hands had cuts and bruises on them. He was drawn-looking, his eyes almost black.

Behind me, Gianna and Roza greeted their husbands, but my attention was on Matteo. His breathing was too fast, and as I pressed my hand to his chest, he winced.

Geo approached us. "Matteo, I need to check you over."

"Look at Alex and Vince first. Marcus needs some stitches," Matteo ordered. "I'm going upstairs. When you finish with them, come see me."

Marcus's voice rang out. "No, Matteo, you were hit the hardest with the blast."

Blast?

Matteo's eyes flashed. "I said the men first. No arguing." He turned, tugging me along with him.

In our room, Matteo sat on the bed, holding me close. His grip was so tight, I knew he would leave marks. I managed to lean back, cupping his face.

"Matteo, tell me."

He crushed me close again, not speaking.

"Tell me what you need."

He stood suddenly, pushing me away. "I need to get these clothes off and shower. I don't want to touch you while I'm in them."

I headed to the bathroom, turning on the shower, confused. He was acting so strangely. He followed me, staying close.

I turned. "Take off your clothes, and I'll have them cleaned."

He did as I instructed, and I gasped when I saw the bruise on his torso, dark and ominous-looking, spreading across his sternum and around his back.

"Matteo," I whispered.

"It looks worse than it is," he assured me. "Shower with me," he pleaded. "I need you close, Evie."

Inside the glass enclosure, he dropped his head to my shoulder, his lips ghosting my ear. "Your bracelet suits you."

"It's beautiful. I love it so much."

He bent, covered my mouth, and kissed me, yanking me tight to him. His actions were forceful, almost desperate. His lips bruised mine, his touch too firm and unyielding. I felt his erection hard against my skin.

"Please, Matteo," I begged. "Tell me what is wrong."

"I need you. I need to be inside you."

My voice faltered as he shoved his leg roughly between mine. "You're h-hurting me," I whispered.

He froze. Then slowly, he stepped back, and his grip loosened. He didn't look at me.

"I'm sorry, Evie."

I cupped his face, forcing his gaze to meet mine. "I'm not asking you to stop, but you need to let me in." I stroked his face. "Was it terrible?"

"Yes."

"Worse than you feared?"

He swallowed, then nodded. "Yes."

"You need to lose yourself with me?"

"Please."

"Then have me. But be *my* Matteo."

With a groan, he wrapped me in his arms again, his mouth on mine. But this time, I felt his tenderness, his yearning. As he stroked my tongue with his, my passion built. His hands soothed over my body, coaxing and gentle. I strained to get closer, my own need building. I caressed his back, gripped his ass, and ran my hands over his taut neck muscles until I felt him give in to the moment.

Finally, he lifted me, and I wrapped my legs around his waist.

"Yes," I murmured.

He slipped inside, burying his face into my neck as he began to move. He didn't thrust and fuck me against the wall the way I expected. His hips circled, keeping us pressed together. He rocked and moved in an easy rhythm until we were both gasping. I cried out his name, and he clutched me close, my name falling from his lips as he climaxed. I shuddered around him, feeling his body jerk with spasms. Then he stilled, holding me tight, not moving.

I kissed his head. "Let me take care of you."

He set me on my feet and allowed me to push him under the hot water. He hunched over so I could wash his hair, careful to avoid the cut. He allowed me to soap his body and cleanse him. Then he did the same for me. No words were spoken, but we shared gentle kisses, and I felt his love in his caresses.

After, we dried off, and I led him to our room. He looked exhausted, letting me push him onto the chair. I was grateful when a soft knock came at the door, and I let Geo in.

I stood to the side as he examined Matteo, clucking at the bruising on his chest, adding butterfly strips to the cut along his head. "That's going to leave a scar," he muttered.

"My wife will overlook it," Matteo replied, meeting my eyes. I could still feel his anxiety, and when he held out his hand, I took it and sat next to him.

"You're lucky the hit wasn't worse," Geo informed him. "If you'd been any closer..." His voice trailed off. He cleared his throat. "I'd feel better with an X-ray. Maybe a scan just to make sure there is no internal damage."

"I'm fine. It's just sore."

Geo met my eyes, and I squeezed Matteo's hand. "Please," I asked.

Matteo huffed. "Fine. But later. I'm exhausted."

"I'll arrange it."

He stood. "I'll stay and make sure everyone is all right. Get some rest."

Matteo nodded, his eyes shut. After Geo left, I lifted the covers on the bed and called to Matteo.

He didn't protest as I drew the blankets over him. But he reached out, tucking himself to my chest with a long sigh. His head rested under my chin, his arms like vises around me.

"Don't leave. Promise me. I cannot rest if you go."

"I'll be right here."

His warm breath drifted over my skin.

"I love you, Evie."

I kissed his head and ran my fingers up and down his back. I felt him succumb to sleep, his body heavier as he gave in. I closed my eyes in exhaustion, wondering what he would tell me when he woke up.

He jerked awake, instantly tense, calling for me.

"I'm right here, Matteo," I soothed, pulling him back to my chest. "Right here."

He exhaled, his arms a steel cage around me.

"Will you go back to sleep? You've only been resting for a little over an hour."

"No," he replied honestly.

"Will you tell me?"

"Not here. Not in our bed."

"Then let me make you something to eat. We can talk in the kitchen."

"Okay."

I felt his eyes on me the whole time I made him breakfast. He ate in silence and barely touched the food, instead pushing it around his plate. Finally, he gave up and picked up his coffee, sipping.

"Matteo," I prompted.

"It was a sex slave ring." His head fell into his hands. "Children, teenagers. Boys, girls. The most blackhearted of bastards selling children for money. Sending them to a life so depraved, many of them would kill themselves rather than bear it." He slammed his hand on the table. "Some already too far gone for us to help."

I covered his hand. "Tell me."

"I can't, Evie. Please don't ask me to share what I saw. I cannot speak of it to you."

"You need to speak of it to someone, Matteo."

"I will. I do. Julian has a team for us."

"Do you allow them to help?"

He met my eyes. "I will this time. I promise."

"All right." I soothed him by running a hand through his hair. "You saved them, Matteo. So many of them."

He flipped his hand, grasping mine. "There is more, Evie. Something much worse."

I nodded, the naked fear in his eyes terrifying me.

"We got the leaders." He swallowed, struggling with words. "All but one."

"Who?"

"The mastermind. He was prepared. Despite all our precautions, he knew we were coming. He was cornered, but he got away. He had escape routes plotted out."

"I'm sorry. I know you'll keep looking."

He stood, pacing, pulling on his hair. "You don't understand. I have to do more. I need to send you somewhere. Somewhere secret. Somewhere safe."

"What are you talking about?" I gasped. "There can't be any place safer than here with you."

"Not anymore!" he roared.

"You aren't making any sense." My voice broke. "W-why are you sending me away, Matteo?"

"I have to make sure you're safe and protected."

I shook my head. "I don't know what's going on. But there is no place safer than close to you."

He dropped in front of me, holding my face. "I don't want to let you go, but I have to. I have no choice."

"Why?" I pleaded with him, tears beginning to gather in my eyes. "I don't understand."

His voice was rough. "Evie, he knew me. He said my name. Your name. He made sure I was the one who followed him. He waited for me to taunt me. He told me I would regret what I had done. He said I had taken away everything of value to him, and he was going to do the same to me."

Our eyes locked.

"He had a trap set. A bomb meant to distract and hurt as he got away. We retreated, but we still took hits from the blast. He told me he was going to take you away from me. The last thing he said to me was I would never find you, and he would make sure you paid for my interference."

My breath caught in my throat at the despair and torment in his expression.

"I have no choice, Evie. I have to let you go."

I stared up at him in disbelief.

Let me go?

A voice startled us both.

"Matteo. Stop this madness. You're frightening Evie."

Matteo sprang to his feet, pivoting, his arms thrown open in a protective gesture. Geo stood in the doorway, Julian behind him. Geo lifted his hands in supplication.

"Relax, Matteo. It's only us."

Matteo's arms dropped.

I had only met Julian once. I had been surprised to see he was Matteo's age. I had expected someone with so much responsibility to be older. He was tall, with dark hair, a short beard, vivid hazel eyes, and his shoulders were broad. He was muscular and incredibly fit and strong. He had been polite and kind when he met me, but I didn't know him very well. His being here made me nervous.

They entered the room. I stood and offered them coffee, which they accepted. They sat, indicating Matteo should as well. Before I could take a seat, Matteo pulled me onto his lap, his grip tight.

Geo sipped his coffee.

Julian frowned. "I know what's happened is upsetting, but sending your wife away is not the answer, Matteo." He indicated the house with a sweep of his hand. "She couldn't possibly be more protected than she is here."

"Upsetting?" Matteo hissed. "*Upsetting*? That fucking lowlife knew my name. He knew about my wife! He *told* me he is coming after her. I will do everything I can to protect her. I can't even imagine what he'd do if…" His voice trailed off, and a shudder went through him, his arms tightening. "I can't risk her."

"It's not going to happen," Julian assured him. "Until he is caught—and he will be caught, Matteo—you're staying here with Evie. All of your people are on guard. You'll be surrounded. Raoul is alone. We've cut off his finances. His people. His network. You killed everyone else in his organization, so he has no one to fall back on. No one he trusts. He isn't going to get to Evie or to you."

He took a drink of his coffee. "Not that he won't try. But we'll be waiting. Separating you from Evie would give him the advantage. Make him come to you. To divide is not to conquer here."

Matteo was silent.

I turned to him. "Please listen to Julian. I can't be away from you, Matteo. I can't."

Geo spoke. "I suggest we all remain here. Safety in numbers. We go about our lives as usual, but we will all be extra cautious." He scrubbed his face, looking as weary as I felt. "I do suggest you stay close to the house, though, Evie. I know it's difficult and you hate being locked away, but for the time being, it is the wisest course of action."

"Even if Marcus goes with me?"

Matteo sighed, his breath warm on my neck. "Even then."

"What about groceries and other things?"

"We'll have them picked up by my men."

"What about Mrs. Armstrong?"

Julian met my eyes. "Anyone Matteo cares about will be protected. She will be fine."

I turned back to Matteo. His brow was furrowed, lines of worry etched around his eyes.

"Please, Matteo," I murmured. "Don't send me away. I couldn't bear it."

His expression softened at my words. "I don't want you to go, Evie."

"You won't send me away, then?"

He groaned, the sound low and tortured. "No."

"Good. We'll protect each other."

He held me close. "Okay."

CHAPTER SEVENTEEN

Evie

I huffed in frustration, shutting the cupboard door. I was out of Matteo's favorite peanut butter, and I knew he'd frown upon me sending someone to the store for a single item. I had sent them only yesterday for groceries, but I'd forgotten to check the jar. Matteo ate a lot of peanut butter.

I headed down the hall to Matteo's office, walking in after rapping on the door, not waiting for Matteo to tell me to enter. Matteo glanced up from his computer, frowning at my annoyed expression.

"Evie, what is it?"

"We're out of peanut butter."

"I'll survive without it."

I squared my shoulders. "I can go to the store with one of your men to get it. There are a few other things I want as well."

He laid down the pen he was holding. "No."

I stepped closer, ignoring the stares of his team.

"Yesterday when Julian was here, he said he was certain they had tracked Raoul to Mexico. He isn't going to turn up at the grocery store and attack me while I get peanut butter."

Matteo stood, his hands clenched in fists on his desk. "I said no."

I crossed my arms, suddenly angry. "Perhaps I am not asking permission, Matteo."

His eyes narrowed, and he raised his hand. "Everyone out."

I heard the door shut behind me and felt a shiver of fear run down my spine, but I refused to let Matteo see my trepidation.

"Julian himself felt Raoul was too busy trying to stay alive and ahead of them to think about coming here. It's been a month of being trapped in this house, unable to do anything." I raised my voice. "I hate it. I need to get out—even if it is a trip to the damn grocery store!"

Matteo's eyebrows shot up, and he studied me while stroking his chin. "Once again, you are surprising me, Evie. I would never have believed you would ever dare to defy me."

I raised my chin. "I promised I would stay close and allow you to ensure my safety. I do not wish to defy you, but you're driving me crazy." My voice broke. "All I want is—is to buy you some damn peanut butter and get a few personal items. Send four men with me if you want, but please let me out of this damn house."

His face softened. "I wish only for your safety. I keep you here because I love you."

I dared to cross the room and stand before him. I cupped his cheek, and he leaned into my caress, turning his face to kiss my palm.

"I hate the fact that you're miserable," he murmured. "I hate keeping you in a cage and living in fear."

"Who do you trust the most to protect me?"

"Me," he replied instantly.

"And to protect you?"

"Marcus."

"Then you come with me and bring Marcus. Add another car of men if you want."

I could see he was wavering.

"Julian was right yesterday when he said we couldn't live like this forever, Matteo. Please. It's only a trip to the store."

He pondered my words, then nodded. "Fine. Marcus drives us, and we go to one store."

"Two."

"You're trying my patience, Evie."

"Matteo, please."

He sighed heavily. "I would give you the world if you asked me, but this is what you request instead. To leave the safety of the estate and put yourself at risk."

I rolled my eyes. "Julian has pictures of Raoul in *Mexico*, Matteo. Thousands of miles from here. I doubt he can see the future and somehow know I'd be out gallivanting and looking for peanut butter today."

His lips twitched. "This isn't a laughing matter."

"I know. But the bottom line is we can't stay cooped up forever. Everyone else has gone back to their lives. I realize they're being extra cautious, but they are still back to their own routines. At some point, you have to allow me to do so as well."

"Until he is caught or dead, you do not leave this house without me knowing and full security, do you understand?"

"But we can go today? Now?"

"Yes."

I flung my arms around his neck, kissing him passionately. He gripped my hips, drawing me flush to him. "Perhaps in a few minutes?" he teased against my lips.

"No. You'll change your mind." I stepped back, tugging his hand. "Now."

He let me lead him out of his office.

"Evie."

I looked up at the sound of Matteo's voice. He stood in the doorway of my craft room, peering in as if afraid to step inside. "Well, you've been busy."

Unable to leave the house, I had filled the freezers with food, swam until I felt I was waterlogged, watched more movies than I had viewed in my entire life, worked with the women, and still had time on my hands. So, I kept busy making things. Wreaths, decorated pinecones, garlands, all sorts of things for the upcoming season filled the room. It was months away, but I would be ready.

"How many houses do you plan to decorate, Evie?" he asked with a grin.

"As many as it takes," I replied. "Do you need something?"

"Julian is here and would like to see both of us," Matteo informed me, turning serious.

Instantly, my nerves kicked in. "Is it bad news?"

He held out his hand. "I hope not. Come with me, please."

We sat in the kitchen around the table. I stared at Julian after he informed us that Raoul Carmen was dead.

Matteo ran a hand through his hair. "Are you certain?"

Julian pushed a pile of photos toward him. "We confirmed Raoul was in the building. Heat imaging showed he was the only one in the room. He had the place wired, which is his MO. There was gunfire, and we found a body. It was identified as his. He's dead, Matteo."

Matteo flipped through the photos, peering hard at the images. "DNA proof?"

"That will take a few days. But it's simply a formality. Look for yourself, Matteo. It's him."

"It looks like him." Matteo grimaced. "A dirty, emaciated shell of him anyway."

"He's been on the run—what did you expect? There was a visual confirmation of him going into the building. Another one of him entering the apartment. Our men were everywhere once we got the tip. He never left, and there was only one body found after the shootout. His."

I didn't look at the pictures. I had no idea what Raoul Carmen looked like, and I didn't care. He was dead.

That meant Matteo would relax. Life would go back to being normal—or at least, as normal as it could be with Matteo. It had been six weeks of being stuck in this house. Aside from two fast trips out to the store, I hadn't been able to get Matteo to relax his constant vigilance.

But the threat was gone now. It was time to move on. And given the news I planned to share later with him, it would be a double cause for celebration.

Julian stood, taking the file folder. "I'll have the DNA results in a few days, so you can relax, Matteo. We can discuss the next case after this is done."

Matteo had been home a lot. He was gone only a day or two, and when he was away, I was surrounded by security, and he checked in frequently. His overprotectiveness made me nervous since I was worried that I was a distraction and he could get hurt because of it again. He had healed well, although the scar on his head was a constant reminder of what had occurred. He had started wearing his hair over his forehead to hide it since he knew it bothered me. He assured me on more than one occasion that he was capable of handling multiple tasks and I shouldn't worry so much. But I did. I had to admit I liked having him home more. What he did was dangerous and risky, but I understood why he did it, even if I didn't like it.

Matteo walked Julian to the door and returned to the kitchen. I slid a cup of coffee toward him, letting him sip the beverage and think about what Julian had told him. Finally, he spoke.

"Nothing changes until DNA is confirmed, Evie. Plus, I want to know for certain no one is taking up his cause. We're still being cautious."

"I understand."

"Once I'm comfortable, Marcus can start taking you for errands again."

I sighed and ran a hand through my hair, pushing the heavy mass off my face. "Matteo, it's been months. No one is looking for me from my old life. No one is threatening me in my new life. Could I not start going out on my own?"

"There are still risks. The answer is no." His look gentled. "You know how much I love you, my wife. I need to protect you."

"Will you ever ease up on this?"

"Perhaps. But not right now."

I knew when not to push him. "Fine. We'll discuss it later." I stood. "I'm going to make dinner. I'd like a quiet evening with my more-relaxed husband, if that is possible."

He caught me around the waist as I walked past, pulling me to his lap. He kissed me—long, hard, and zealously. "I love your feisty side, Evie. I love that you challenge me, even if it pisses me off at times."

I returned his kisses happily.

"I like challenging you. Someone has to."

He laughed and kissed the end of my nose. "Things will get better now. Once this is one hundred percent confirmed, I promise I will relax."

I played with the hair at the back of his neck. He loved it when I did that. "Good. I need you relaxed."

"Oh?"

My stomach fluttered a little as I took his hand and laid it over my abdomen. "I understand being a father is stressful enough."

He frowned, confused. "Being a father? I'm not..." His eyes widened, and he looked down at his hand. "Evie, are you...*am I*...are we?"

I nodded. "Yes, I'm pregnant. With everything going on, I realized I missed my shot. I had to have a test before I get it again, and Geo confirmed I was pregnant." I paused. "Are you angry?"

"Angry? Absolutely not. Stunned, perhaps. You were unsure about children. How do you feel about it?"

I had told him my fears, and he had assured me he wanted children. Especially with me. He told me a family was something he had longed for since he'd lost his parents. He'd said when I was ready, we could discuss the future. And that if I chose not to have children, he would understand. But he had looked so sad at the thought.

"I was scared at first, then I realized how excited I was."

"Tell me again, Evie." He spread his fingers wide over my stomach.

I cupped his cheek. "You're going to be a daddy, Matteo, and we're going to be parents."

His face broke into a smile. A real one. His eyes shone, and his joy was evident. His kiss was filled with love. "Evie, my wife. First, the news Raoul is not a threat to you, and now this? You just made this day the best one of my life."

He stood, swinging me up into his arms.

"What are you doing?" I gasped. "Put me down."

He strode from the kitchen, heading for the stairs. "No. I am taking my wife, my beautiful, pregnant wife, upstairs. I am going to run her a warm bath, rub her shoulders, and we are going to make plans for the future—about our child and our life together. Then, I'm going to make love to her until she is totally sated."

I snuggled into his chest, feeling happiness and relief flooding through me. "That might take a while."

He grinned down at me. "I was hoping it would."

CHAPTER EIGHTEEN

Evie

"One hundred percent? We're confident?" Matteo frowned as he flipped through the papers.

Julian shook his head. "What else can I give you to prove it, Matteo? It's his DNA. Raoul is dead."

A rush of relief flooded me. This was the news we'd been waiting for. I watched Matteo process the information. Slowly, the realization of Julian's words sank in, and Matteo's expression cleared.

"The threat is over."

"Yes. Your team, your wife, and your identity are safe."

Matteo met my eyes, his relief blatant. His gaze dropped to my stomach, then lifted back to my eyes. I knew what he was thinking. His family was safe. That was paramount to him. We had become more important than his work. More important than anything. I knew it without a doubt. Our gazes locked and held. Love blazed from his eyes as he looked at me, and he nodded slightly.

He sat back in his chair. "This is good news, Julian. Thank you." He inhaled a deep breath. "And I have some news for you as well. I'm leaving the squad."

The entire room, myself included, stared in shock. Marcus, Alex, Vince, and Geo were in the room with us, all anxious for the confirmation of Raoul's death. They were as surprised as I was at his words.

"Matteo," Julian protested. "You can't be serious."

"I am. Things have changed, Julian. My life, my priorities have changed. Next time, I might not be so lucky, and Evie, *my family*, is too important for me to risk. If Raoul knew my name, he could have passed that information along to someone else. I can't take the risk. It might jeopardize the team and what we do. It only makes sense."

Julian shook his head in disbelief. "Matteo…"

Matteo's voice dropped, his face serious. "It isn't only about me anymore."

Julian frowned.

"Evie is pregnant, Julian. I have to protect her at all costs."

I felt every eye in the room on me. After a long silence, Julian huffed out a sigh.

"Matteo, this division, this team, will be lost without you."

"No. Marcus can do this. He's the obvious choice. The men respect him, and he'll do an outstanding job. He is exactly who you need to lead the team." Matteo paused. "He can give you one hundred percent of himself, Julian. I no longer have that to give."

Julian's shoulders slumped. "I understand. I always knew this day would come." He lifted his shoulder with a small smile. "I'd hoped I would have been retired before it happened. But I'm happy for you, Matteo." Julian smiled and leaned forward, extending his hand. "For you both. Congratulations."

Matteo shook his hand with a nod. "We can discuss this in private later and figure it all out."

Geo walked Julian to the door.

Marcus stood, his expression serious. "Matteo, I am honored you think I can lead this team, but…" His voice trailed off.

Matteo shook his head. "No buts, Marcus. You're the right man. I discussed this a long time ago with Alex and Vince. They both agreed, when the time came, you were the one to step into my shoes."

Alex and Vince nodded in agreement.

"I plan to step back myself in a few years," Vince stated. "But until I do, I agree with Matteo. You're the man to lead us."

Marcus glanced toward me, and I smiled. I knew how much Matteo trusted him and how highly he thought of Marcus. We had become close, and there was no doubt Matteo had chosen well.

"You'll be a great leader," I assured him.

He frowned, muttered his excuses, and left the room. Like Matteo, he always needed a little time to think things over when it came to something that affected him on a personal level. When it came to what they did, the lives they saved, and the risks they took, their decision-making process was instant and unquestionable.

Matteo glanced at me and looked toward Alex and Vince. They stood and left the room. Geo rose to follow.

"I'll give you some privacy, but this evening, we are celebrating this. All of it. The end of this chapter and the beginning of your new life, Matteo. I'm so happy for you both." He pulled the door closed behind him.

Matteo crossed over and crouched beside me.

"Are you all right, Evie?"

I cupped his cheek. "I'm fine. A little surprised. Are you sure about this, Matteo?"

He met my inquisitive gaze with a look of determination. "Yes. I've been thinking about it for a while." He placed his hand on my stomach, rubbing it lovingly. "Our child needs a world free from all of this madness. From the danger it brings to our life. I want to disappear with you. Start fresh in a place free from blood and fear. I want to live my life in peace with you. With our family."

"But you feel so strongly about this cause."

He nodded. "And it will continue after I leave. After Vince and Alex leave. Julian knew I would go." He sighed. "Eventually, we all have to walk away before it consumes us." He tilted his head to the side, studying me. "I admit, if you hadn't come into my life, I would have gone on for longer. But you awakened parts of me I kept buried. The parts that allow me to feel more than anger and hate and the need for revenge. Now I know Raoul is dead, I can walk away. I want to grab those feelings and live."

"I love you," I whispered.

He smiled. "That is the greatest gift of my life. That and our little one growing inside you. You have brought joy to my life, Evie. And now it's time to move on from the past and into the future. Our future."

"What will happen next?"

He sat across from me, taking my hand. "It will take some time. Things need to be put into place, I need to wind down and make sure Marcus is ready to step in. Julian will need me to ensure the transition is clean."

"Will this house still be the center?"

He shrugged. "That will be up to Marcus. I doubt it. I know he would prefer more distance between the job and his life." He barked out a laugh. "He is already smarter than me."

"What about the fund?"

"That's easy. I think, if Julian is okay with it, we'll still maintain it. I can get involved, and we can still help the team that way, making sure people are looked after."

"So, we stay here?"

"No, I still want to take you away from here. Somewhere safe and quiet. We'll figure it all out. I think, for now, we'll stay here until the baby is born. I know you'll get great care with the doctor Geo has recommended, and he will be close. Then we can decide where we go next."

"All right." I leaned forward, and he met me halfway, our mouths connecting with tenderness. His kiss always made me feel his love. "I like what the future holds."

He kissed me again. "Me too, Evie. Me too."

I pushed some jars aside and peered into the depths of the refrigerator with a dissatisfied groan. I was desperate for grape jelly. On soft, doughy white bread. And a glass of milk.

The problem was it was the same craving I'd had for the past six weeks. Twenty-four hours a day. Matteo had made sure I had several jars of my favorite brand of jelly in the cupboard before he left on another job, but between the cravings and my stress level at his being away, I had eaten it all.

And drank the milk.

I squinted at the clock. It was early—not even seven in the morning. I never slept well when Matteo was gone, and this time was no exception. Even with things winding down, what he did was still dangerous. Despite what he said, I knew he would work until the last day. He assured me he took a back seat to Marcus now, letting him direct the crew, and he was there only as backup and a sounding board, but I still worried.

I shut the door with a huff. Matteo would be home later today, and then I could go to the store and get some more jelly and bread. Or if I texted him, he would stop before getting home. I looked down at my round belly, rubbing it. Even though I was safe, he preferred me not to leave the house without an escort. Preferably him.

"You have to wait, baby girl," I murmured.

As if in protest, there was a little push against my hand. I laughed quietly. "Just like your father—impatient. There is nothing I can do, so you just *have* to be patient."

Matteo had been beside himself with joy when we found out we were having a girl. He showed everyone in the crew the ultrasound picture and framed it, putting it on his desk. He came to every appointment with me, held my hand during tests, rubbed my aching back, and soothed me during the first few months of morning sickness. I think he had rejoiced as much as I did when the first trimester passed and I got my appetite and energy back. He thoroughly enjoyed the other appetites that came with the second trimester, although at times, he swore I was wearing him out.

Sounds from outside drew me to the window. The grounds crew was already here, working in the gardens. I knew they would wait until after eight to start cutting the grass, but since I was awake, there wasn't really any reason for them to do so. Matteo had only changed that guideline when I became pregnant and he didn't want my sleep interrupted.

I opened the back door and stepped outside. Over the past couple of months, Matteo had relaxed, and once he did, I found myself feeling better. More open and at ease with my life. I made sure to introduce myself to all the workers allowed on the property. I wanted to be part of the daily activity, and I enjoyed talking to them since I had always loved gardening.

Marcus was busy shadowing all of Matteo's moves and getting ready to step into his role. I missed him and our friendship. I had a new bodyguard, Sal, who followed me around, ensuring my safety and that the workers understood exactly who I was. I ignored him for the most part. He was even more intense than Marcus but, despite my efforts to be friendly, remained aloof. Still, I went along, doing what I wanted, getting to know everyone, and causing Sal to huff in frustration.

On occasion, Matteo would call me into his office and ask me to "give Sal a break." But his attempts to hide his grin when he did so let me know he was fine with my behavior. He often kissed me, telling me how proud he was of his wife. The fact that I liked to know the names and people who worked here made him smile. He chuckled at the cases of water and snacks I kept in the shed and handed out when I went to say hello to them. But I noticed how often he would appear by his window, observing me as I went around chatting and making sure everyone was hydrated. He was ever watchful, and I liked knowing he took the time to make sure I was all right.

I knew Sal was in the house. I had heard him earlier. Unlike Marcus, he checked on me rather than constantly being beside me. I preferred it, given our more distant relationship. Sal would work in the office until Matteo arrived home, and then he would leave unobtrusively. There were men outside, but I rarely saw them. They watched the house from another building, making sure the grounds were safe. I was looking forward to the day when it was only Matteo and me and our family.

As it was, it was only Sal and me today, as Roza and Lila were having a shopping day. Gianna and Vince were out on their own for a rare excursion outside the gates. I had used my exhaustion as an excuse not to go. I wanted to be home when Matteo arrived, and I was too tired to walk much. The rest of Matteo's men were with him.

I stepped outside, breathing in the fresh air. It was going to be a lovely autumn day, the temperature above normal. I approached the men working in the garden with a smile.

"Good morning!"

They all looked up with smiles as they greeted me. "Good morning, Mrs. Campari."

"It's going to be warm. I have water in the refrigerator and some of those crunchy bars you all love. The door is open to the shed, so please help yourself."

They all thanked me.

My favorite crew member came around the corner. "Hi, Mrs. Campari."

I smiled. "Hi, Tom. Haven't seen you the last couple of weeks."

He shook his head. "Yeah, bit under the weather."

"Well, I hope you're better."

He nodded. "Much. You're up early."

I chuckled, rubbing my stomach. "Someone is kicking. You can start cutting the grass anytime. I'm awake, so you won't disturb me."

"Great."

I sat down with a sigh as the crew started back to work.

"Are you okay, Mrs. Campari?"

I smiled. "Aside from my craving and missing my husband, I'm good."

"Craving?" Tom grinned. "My wife had those bad. What are you wanting?"

"Grape jelly sandwiches on white bread. With gobs of butter."

He laughed. "Are your supplies low?"

"Empty."

"Oh, that's bad news."

I nodded.

"I'll run and pick up some for you."

"I can't ask you to do that."

He waved his hand. "You didn't—I offered. Jack won't mind. I'll run to the store, grab the stuff, and be back in ten minutes." He studied me earnestly. "My wife would expect me to help out another pregnant woman."

I hesitated. Tom was a newer addition to the crew. He wasn't always here, but I liked him. He had helped me one day when I stumbled, reaching out to steady me with a knowing grin, explaining his wife had the same trouble now that she was "top-heavy" too.

We had started talking, and I discovered he was intelligent and kind. He was missing two fingers on one hand—a "hazard of the job" he had told me when I finally got up the courage to ask him.

"I learned to handle all the equipment again. But I prefer the actual work. I love digging in the dirt. There is something very satisfying about planting and nurturing things," he said in his quiet voice.

He spoke of his wife a lot, and I enjoyed our conversations. Bald with dark eyes, he wore hats most of the time and worked hard. He never approached me if Matteo or Marcus were around, and I had a feeling they intimidated him. He seemed quite shy, and I could understand his feelings.

"Please, Mrs. Campari. It's not a problem."

I gave in. I was desperate. "Okay. Let me get you the money."

He followed me into the kitchen, waiting by the door.

"Darn it, my purse is in the hall. I'll be right back."

"Sure."

I hurried as fast as I could and returned to the kitchen with some cash. He was in the same spot, looking around with curiosity. "My wife would love this kitchen."

"It's a nice one," I agreed and handed him the money.

"I'll be back fast. Okay if I go through the garage to the truck?"

"Sure. You're a lifesaver."

"No problem."

He came back in about fifteen minutes, knocking on the garage door. I opened it with a smile. "I didn't hear the truck."

"I parked farther down the driveway." He carried the bag to the counter. "I got Smuckers, like you asked." He held up the jar.

I reached for it. "Thank you."

He smiled. "No problem, Mrs. Campari. Enjoy your sandwiches."

He slipped out the door, and I made my sandwich, sighing in satisfaction as I bit through the soft bread. I ate two sandwiches, drank a tall glass of milk, and sat back, replete.

"Better, baby?" I asked quietly, running my hand over my stomach. I looked around the kitchen with a smile. "Now if only Daddy would get home, it would be perfect." I yawned, feeling sleepy. "Maybe a nap would help pass the time."

A couple of hours later, after a nap and a shower, I dressed in a pretty skirt and blouse, wanting to look nice for Matteo when he got home later. I loved the skirt with its lace trim and deep pockets—I often carried a snack in one, which made Matteo chuckle.

Humming, I walked into the kitchen, startling when I saw Tom sitting at the table. I frowned in confusion.

"Tom?"

"Mrs. Campari."

I looked around, unsure. "Are you all right?"

"Yes."

"I thought I heard the crew leave."

"They did."

A shiver of fear ran down my spine. He was staring at me, the usual friendly expression on his face gone. Instead, his face was impassive, blank. Even his voice was different. It was no longer soft or shy. It was cold.

I began to back up, and he stood. "Don't bother. Sal can't help you." He tilted his head. "No one can help you."

"Wh–what?"

"I've been waiting for this. I knew it was only a matter of time until you showed exactly how stupid you were."

My gaze tore around the room. I didn't know what was happening. I didn't understand.

"St–stupid?" I repeated.

"Letting me into your house. That was all I needed. But then you gave me a gift. A minute alone in your kitchen. All it took was thirty seconds, and I had everything I needed."

"Needed?"

He held up his hand. A small gadget sat in his palm. "I have every code. Every door is locked. Every camera belongs to me. I control everything." His smile terrified me. "I control you."

"I–I…"

"Let me introduce myself properly." Another dark smile curled his mouth. "After all, you should know the name of the man who is going to bring your husband to his knees." From behind his back, he withdrew a gun.

My mouth opened, but no words came out.

"Raoul. My name is Raoul Carmen. And I'm going to kill you. Very slowly."

His evil smile grew.

"And let your husband watch."

CHAPTER NINETEEN

Evie

I stood frozen with fear, his words echoing in my head.

"Kill you. Slowly."

"Let your husband watch."

The man I knew as Tom smiled coldly as he watched my growing terror, my hand flying to my stomach in a defensive gesture.

"But–but Julian said you were dead. They had your DNA…"

He held up his hand, the gap of his missing fingers suddenly telling a different story. "A small price to pay." He shrugged. "A dead body that looked like me, some donated blood and body parts, and an easily bribed lab worker—anything can be made to appear different from what it really is with the right incentive. Like being dead

—or assuming the identity of another living person for a while."

"Is there really a Tom Smith?"

He tilted his head. "There...*was*. Your husband himself approved the application. I got to know Tom well before..." He trailed off, and I knew what he wasn't saying.

I swallowed at his implication.

"He was kind enough to share many stories of his pregnant wife. They proved to be invaluable. I was most grateful."

"And?" I whispered.

"I thanked him by killing them all quickly." He smirked. "They never saw it coming. Most never do. Idiots. They believe what they see—like you."

He waved his hand as if it was no big deal. As if killing people and removing body parts didn't matter.

With growing horror, I knew neither did. He continued as if we were simply discussing the weather.

"This time, I can enjoy it. Take my time. What a treat it will be destroying the only things that matter to your husband. Taking away from him the two things he holds most dear." His smile became so evil it made my knees weak. "I shall have so much pleasure. So worth the wait."

"He'll kill you," I threatened wildly. "He won't stop until he finds you."

He sneered, not even remotely worried. "He will be so overcome by grief and anger he'll be an easy target. Little does he know his hell is only beginning."

"Wh—what?"

"I was going to take you and let him suffer. But it's not enough. I'm going to kill every member of his team, his family, and anyone else I think he might even remotely like. And when he has nothing left and nothing to live for, I'll kill him. Once I think he's suffered *enough* loss." He laughed—the sound so cold I shivered. "And I think he needs to *really* suffer." He slid the gun into his pocket and reached behind him, pulling out a knife. The lethal-looking weapon glinted in the light, traces of blood clinging to the blade.

I gripped the back of the chair to stop myself from falling. I could feel the color draining from my face, and my stomach clenched. I slapped my hand over my mouth and rushed to the sink, dry heaving over the edge as panic seized me. Hot tears spilled down my cheeks, and my breath came out in loud gasps.

I cried out as Raoul grabbed my arm, his grip brutal. He dragged me from the kitchen, down the hall, and into Matteo's office. Sal was on the floor, surrounded by a pool of blood. It was obvious he had fought hard but lost. I pushed down the nausea, turning my head, and silently apologized to him. We weren't close the way

Marcus and I were, but he had died trying to protect me. I owed him that much.

Raoul shoved me into Matteo's chair, leaning over me and typing on the keyboard, opening up a screen.

"Does your wife know what you do?" I asked, thinking of all the stories he had told me.

He laughed again. "You are so gullible. I have no wife. I knew if I told you bullshit about 'my own family,' you would relax and trust me." He shook his head. "It was all I could do not to kill you the first time I saw you, but this is so much better. Even if it was a pain having to disguise myself as someone else and avoid your husband and that fucking asshole of a bodyguard you had on you all the time." He leaned closer. "Just for the record, I fucking hate working in the dirt too. You have to pay for all that. You and your fucking Matteo." He pushed a few more keys, opening the camera on Matteo's computer.

"Call him."

"No," I said bravely. He could kill me, but I refused to make Matteo watch.

He slapped me so hard, I saw stars, and my lip broke open, the blood dripping on my chin. "Message him with video on, or I'll kill your child first." He pressed the gun to my stomach. "I can do that and keep you alive."

My hands shook as I tapped Matteo's number. He answered after only one ring, and with a sinking heart, I realized this would be the last time I saw him. His face filled the screen.

"Hello, my wife. Need something?" he teased. "Grape jelly, perhaps?" Then his expression changed as he saw me. "Evie? What happened to your face?"

I tried to speak, but I couldn't. Tears welled, pouring down my face. I choked on the fear filling my throat.

"Evie! Baby, what is it? Get Sal!" His voice became panicked, then he gasped, shocked as Raoul stepped behind me.

"Hello, Matteo."

My head pounded, my throat tight, as I watched all the color drain from Matteo's face. I saw Marcus step behind him briefly, then disappear. Raoul laughed.

"Tell your sidekick whatever he thinks he's going to start won't work. I have control, Matteo. The outside men are dead, and so is the useless bodyguard. I have your wife, and I have the codes for every door, lock, and gate in this house. Every code that has been used in the past three months has been canceled. No one can get in." He leaned forward, running the knife down my cheek. "And no one can get out."

"Whatever you want is yours. Anything," Matteo said. "Just let her go. She is innocent in all this."

"Would you trade your life for hers?"

Matteo didn't hesitate. "Yes."

"Too bad I'm not interested."

"I have millions. It's all yours. Every cent. You can disappear and start over." Matteo stood, holding his phone, pacing the way he did when upset. His voice was tight but calm, although I could see the panic in his eyes. His gaze would dart to the side then back to the phone, and I knew his mind was racing to come up with solutions. I could hear shouting and see he was moving, then the sound of a car door slamming. He was trying to get to me, but I knew it was too late.

"Oh, I'll get your money. But first, you have to suffer."

A muffled sob escaped my lips. Matteo held the phone close, his voice low and gentle. "It's okay, Evie. It will all be okay. I promise you."

Raoul leaned down, chuckling. "Listen to him lie. He knows nothing is going to be okay. He knows you're going to die, but the best part is coming." He pushed me out of the way, filling the camera. "The best part, Matteo, is you get to watch. Everything I do to her. Every painful slice of my knife, slap of my hand, skim of my bullet—you get to witness."

Matteo lost it. He began shouting obscenities, screaming at Raoul, who listened, calm and detached, studying the knife he held in his hand. One he planned to use on me. I looked at the monitors surrounding the property. A car went by slowly, followed by another. I wasn't sure if they were here because they had been sent or were simply driving past, admiring the estate. It didn't matter. The thick walls and unclimbable gate that had been designed to keep the occupants inside safe would work against them. If Sal was dead and Raoul had killed the other men who patrolled the perimeter of the grounds, I was alone and trapped. Raoul was going to kill me and my child, and I would never see Matteo again. Never feel his mouth on mine or hear his voice.

"Your sister will be next," Raoul announced. "I'll let her relive her teenage horror once I kill Vince. Shame they weren't home earlier. But their turn will come. Anyone and everyone you care about is going to die."

"You goddamn coward," Matteo sneered, not reacting to his statement. "Killing innocents and thinking you're better than them. Than me."

"Oh, I don't think it. I know it. I hate weakness. It deserves to be exploited."

"It deserves to be protected from scum like you."

"Oh, Matteo," Raoul sneered. "Are you trying to hurt my feelings?" He leaned closer to the screen. "News flash, you stupid idiot. I have none."

He leaned back, almost relaxed. "At least, that was what a psychiatrist told me once. I corrected him after I slit his throat. I assured him I thoroughly enjoyed watching him die."

He grabbed the arm of the chair, pushing me into the desk. "Say goodbye to your husband, little Evie."

My knee hit the hidden gun holder, my hand fumbling as I realized it was empty. Raoul shook his head, his voice filled with false pity.

"Nice try. I found the gun." He held it up. "It will amuse me knowing I used the gun he kept to protect you to kill you once I'm ready." His face turned dark. "It might take me a while to be satisfied, though."

I leaned close to the screen, fumbling as quietly as I could to try to find the second gun. I had no idea how good a shot I was, but I would try. Matteo continued to curse and yell orders.

"Matteo, I love you!" I cried, needing those to be the last words he heard from me.

My voice stopped his tirade. "Evie," he rasped. "Fight him. Give me a chance to get to you."

"How touching," Raoul mocked. "But Matteo is right. You deserve a chance." He sat down, crossing his legs. "I fancy a bit of a game. Hide-and-seek. I'm going to give you ten seconds to hide, then I'm going to find you, and my enjoyment will begin. Won't that be fun?"

"What?" I asked, dumbfounded.

He leaned forward. "You must be a good fuck because you are pitifully stupid. I said run. Hide. You have ten seconds." He sat back. "In fact, I'll give you twenty, given your *delicate* condition. Only in the house, I'm afraid." He patted his pocket. "I have control of the codes now. The outside doors won't work, so no one can join us."

I heard Marcus's voice behind Matteo.

"Evie! Think about the Post-its!"

Something twigged in my fear-induced mind, and I grappled with figuring it out. A word repeated in my head.

Codes.

Codes.

It clicked.

Codes.

Raoul said three months. Any code used in the past three months was locked out. There was one code that hadn't been used for a longer period than that.

And I knew exactly where to find it.

I drew in a deep breath.

He lifted one eyebrow, ignoring Matteo's cursing and threats. Raoul held the knife up to the light.

"One," he said.

I slid the gun into the pocket of my voluminous skirt.

And I ran.

CHAPTER TWENTY

Evie

I raced through the kitchen, one arm wrapped around my stomach protectively. The door into the garage was the only one that didn't require a code. It opened with a key from the outside and inside, and I always had one in my pocket. It was another one of Matteo's rules in case of fire. I lost a few precious beats trying to get the key into the lock, but I was able to pull the door open and I ran like hell. I could already hear Raoul bearing down on me. In the garage, I ducked between the cars, with one target in mind. At the far end sat Mrs. Armstrong's car—unused since Marcus had backed it in.

He never canceled her code. The keys were left in the car the same way she always did. Matteo laughed at that, saying no one would ever steal the little Toyota over the rest of his luxury cars, and it saved everyone time when she misplaced them once again.

If I could get to the car and start it, I could get out. At least as far as the gate, where I could cause a scene and buy myself some time.

I heard Raoul enter the garage. "Nice try, Evie. You can't get out. But there are certainly a lot of items in here I can use to punish you."

I risked peeking over the edge of a car. Raoul was holding up his phone, now streaming his hunt of me to torture Matteo.

I refused to allow that to happen. Ignoring the pain it caused me, I crawled on the floor, scraping my knees, carefully edging my way toward the far side. I knew Raoul was strolling through the garage, not concerned, giving Matteo a running commentary on all the things he was going to do to me when he caught me. I tried to shut out his vile, terrifying words, allowing my tears to fall soundlessly as I attempted to escape. I had almost gotten to the car when he appeared behind me, yanking me up by my hair, causing me to cry out at the pain in my scalp. He began to drag me toward the large worktable at the back, and I remembered some self-defensive things Marcus had taught me.

"Use the element of surprise, Evie. Always."

Raoul tossed me toward the workbench, and I grabbed the edge, preventing myself from hitting full force. He set down his phone, and I took the split second his concentration was off me to grab the heaviest item on the table. When he turned back, I swung the wrench, striking his head.

It was his turn to howl in pain.

He let me go, and I ran, pulling the gun from my pocket. I turned and pulled the trigger, my hand shaking so hard I wasn't sure where my aim was directed.

There was another scream behind me, one of shock and pain as well as rage, and I knew I had hit him somewhere. I didn't care where—I just wanted it to slow him down.

I took advantage and began to run straight for the car. I was inside, with the doors locked, just as he grabbed the handle. He glared at me, lowering his face to the window.

"You just made this ten times worse on yourself, you bitch. Open the door, and I'll forget this happened."

"Fuck you," I yelled and, with a silent prayer, turned the key. The engine sputtered, then roared to life. Raoul began to laugh. "What are you going to do? Crash this car into the garage door? It's reinforced bulletproof steel! You can't get through it, you stupid woman." He sneered, then lifted his gun. "Those windows aren't bulletproof, though. Turn it off and get the fuck out of the car."

I knew the six-digit number by heart—654654—they had always tried to keep her code easy. I punched the numbers into the remote, Raoul laughing at what he conceived to be my stupid attempt to escape him. He held his shoulder where the bullet I had fired must have struck him. Blood seeped through his shirt, and I hoped it hurt like hell.

The garage door began to roll upward, and Raoul's laughter stopped as he gaped at the entrance, then began to run toward the panel, and I knew he intended to override the code. I shifted into drive, stepping on the gas. The tires squealed, and the car shot forward so fast, I could barely control it. The door stopped, beginning to shut again, and I closed my eyes, letting the car go forward, deciding I would rather die this way than let him hurt us. The car burst through the gap, the bottom of the large garage door scraping the roof, the sound loud and wrenching. I kept going. I got to the gate, and I flung open the door and began screaming. Bullets whizzed past me, and I ran blindly, heading for the trees, zigzagging to put off Raoul's aim. I felt as if I were in a tunnel, confused and dazed. There seemed to be so much noise. Screaming and shouting, the sounds of metal on metal. Angry voices filled my head, and I had no idea if my fear was causing me to hallucinate, but I couldn't stop to figure it out.

Burning pain, vivid and sharp, tore through my chest, sending me sprawling. Blood seeped from the hole as I lay on the ground, my gasps ringing in my ears. There were more shouts and screams, loud obscenities, and gunshots as I curled up, holding my stomach, the life draining from me. Darkness edged in as I cradled my baby, hoping Matteo would survive when he got here.

That he would somehow pick up his life and carry on. I prayed that, by some miracle, our daughter would live, giving Matteo the strength to carry on. He would protect her. Love her.

I heard my name being shouted, and I stayed still, allowing the darkness to take over. If I was dead when Raoul found me, he couldn't hurt Matteo or me anymore.

The feel of gentle hands and the sound of a voice filled with love and worry calling my name were the last things I knew.

The angel who greeted me sounded very much like Matteo.

MATTEO

Fear had been a constant companion since the day my sister disappeared. It ate at me and crawled under my skin daily. Even after she was returned, it never settled. When my parents died in an accident that was meant to take me as well, the fear became a silent, daily companion, never far away, always bubbling near the surface, needing to be tamped down with the only defense I had against it—my own will. I fought daily to never show it.

It reared its ugly head the day Evie went for her shopping trip and again the day I heard her name fall from the lips of the scum Raoul Carmen. Adding loathing to the fear twisted it into a monster I struggled to control.

But nothing prepared me for the agonizing, churning terror of seeing her face on the screen, with the man we thought was dead holding a gun to her head.

The monster roared to life, and I knew with a certainty beyond comprehension, I would kill that man today. I knew the likelihood was I would die trying, but as long as he was extinguished from this world, that was all that mattered.

He was going to take the one thing in my life I would give the world for, so it mattered not if I lived. A world without Evie wasn't a place I wanted to be anymore. She had become the nucleus of my life, and I revolved around her like the earth orbiting the sun. Without her warmth, I would perish anyway.

I listened as that piece of shit followed my wife, his vile words making my stomach churn and my resolve strengthen. The car was already traveling well over the speed limit, dodging other cars and going through traffic lights. We had been getting ready to leave to return home when the call came in from Evie, so we weren't far away. I prayed we got there fast enough. When the shot rang out and I realized it was Evie who shot Raoul and not the other way around, my gaze flew to Marcus.

"Where did she get a gun?" he asked in wonder.

"The second holster under the desk." She had asked me

one day, and I had shown her how it worked, although I made her promise never to touch it. She had remembered, and I was grateful for her cleverness.

Marcus was barking orders into his phone, the car phone, and the spare he carried. All were on speaker. Men were already at the house and the override code being engaged. If Raoul thought I was stupid enough never to plan for this situation, he was more arrogant than I thought. It was probably his greatest weakness.

"We need to go faster," I yelled.

"One minute and we're there."

We arrived to chaos. Mrs. Armstrong's Toyota was by the gates, the driver's side door open. I was out of the car before it stopped moving, Marcus on my heels. My stomach clenched as I saw the scene unfolding in front of me. Evie running, Raoul's feet planted as he took aim at her. I knew he would kill her even with her trying not to go in a straight line. I lifted my gun at the same time Marcus did, both of us moving forward. We fired, hitting the scum just as his gun went off. He pirouetted, his arms thrown up, the shocked look on his face as he fell almost comical. I kept running, shouting at Marcus.

"Make sure he's down! Get an ambulance!"

As I went past, I saw Raoul's chest moving, and without a thought, I lifted my gun and shot him. Repeatedly. His body jerked on the grass, and I kept shooting until the chamber was empty, then tossing the gun away.

Evie was still on the ground, and I dropped to my knees, gathering her in my arms and turning her gently. Blood spread along the left side of her, soaking her shirt and cardigan. I grappled with the image of her in front of me. Of how pale she was. Knowing that if she was gone, if my child was taken as well, this world would no longer hold any place for me. A life without Evie and my daughter was not one I would be able to face.

I began talking, crying, begging all at once, my hands never stopping in their movement over her.

"Don't leave me, Evie. God, don't leave me…"

"I have you, baby. Help is coming. Stay with me…"

"Please, God, don't take her. Please…"

"Evie, open your eyes. I'm here. I love you…"

"You were so brave, baby…"

"Please, God…"

Marcus appeared beside me, pushing my hands out of the way and pulling down her cardigan.

"It's below her shoulder, Matteo." He grabbed my arm. "She's unconscious, not dead."

"The blood," I mumbled, unable to think clearly. "So much blood."

"There always is," he said. "You know that. Listen. The ambulance is here. Can you hear it? She's going to be fine. They are *both* going to be fine."

I wasn't sure either of us believed his words. But I held on to them with everything in me.

EVIE

I awoke gradually, my head aching, my body on fire, and the strangest sensation in my arm. My eyes opened, blinking in the dim light. I was surrounded by machines that beeped and whirled. I frowned, confused. Why did heaven look like a hospital room?

I looked over and discovered the source of the strange sensation. Matteo was asleep, his hand wrapped around mine, his cheek resting on my forearm. My arm and hand were numb from the weight of his head. In the corner, Marcus slumbered, his large frame taking up most of the small sofa.

"Am I dreaming?" I asked, my voice low, raspy, and confused.

Matteo's head shot up, and Marcus pushed out of his chair, hurrying toward the door.

"Evie," Matteo whispered, running his hands over my face and arms. "Oh God, *Piccolina*. Thank God you're awake."

"I'm not dead?"

"No." He shook his head. "You're not dead."

Panicked, I looked down, my hand flying to my stomach. Matteo laid his large palm on top of mine. "Our little one is fine, Mommy. We've been waiting for you to wake up."

"How long?" I asked.

"A few days. You hit your head when you fell, and you lost a lot of blood," Matteo explained, his hands still running over me in a constant motion. "The doctor assured me you'd be fine. He said you'd suffered a lot of trauma and your body needed the time to recover." Matteo's eyes glistened in the dim light. "I've been right here, waiting to see your beautiful eyes open for me." He cupped my cheek. "And here you are."

The doctor came in, making Matteo stand back while he examined me. Matteo refused to leave the room, and the doctor didn't argue with him. I had a feeling he'd already had that argument many times. When he finished, a nurse helped me settle a little, then once again, I was alone with Matteo. He never took his eyes off me the entire time, and as soon as he could, he was right back beside me, holding my hand and stroking my cheek.

"Raoul?" I asked fearfully.

"Dead," Marcus stated, walking in. "For real this time. I put the bullet between his eyes myself just to be sure."

I shuddered, and Matteo leaned down, stroking my head. "It's all right, Evie. He can't hurt you again. Baby, I'm so sorry. I failed you badly."

"You didn't," I insisted. "We all thought he was dead. None of us knew. I had no idea what he looked like until he told me his name. I thought he was one of the workers. He seemed so nice," I explained. "He told me about his wife and their life." I shook my head. "I believed him."

"That was how he lured all his victims in. He was the consummate actor. He'd get women, children, entire families to trust him, then before they knew what was happening, their lives were gone. They were sold as slaves or worse. He murdered the real Tom and assumed his identity. He was a new crew member, so even his coworkers didn't know him. He planned it all very well." Matteo shook his head. "Raoul was the worst excuse for a human being I ever had to deal with, and his death only benefits the world."

He leaned closer, his voice low. "I hate that he touched you. Hurt you. Threatened you. I loathe the fact that you heard all those vile things he said he was going to do to you."

"I was so scared," I admitted, my voice shaking as the memories swirled in my head.

"You were so brave," Marcus spoke up. "You did exactly what I hoped you would do. You bought us enough time to get to you."

"How did you get in?"

Marcus laughed. "Raoul thought he was so smart, but Matteo is always one step ahead. There was one override code only we had to get in, no matter what. We were pulling up with reinforcements just after you jumped out and started to run. Raoul began shooting wildly at you and us." He looked upset. "A stray bullet got your shoulder."

"And you got him," I said quietly.

"Yes. Four times. Added to Matteo's six, I'm certain he stayed down," Marcus stated dryly.

I looked at Matteo. "You shot him *six* times?"

"He hurt you. If I could have, I would have resuscitated him and done it again. I wanted him so bullet-ridden there was no doubt this time."

I had no reply for that.

Marcus cleared his throat. "I'll leave you two alone. There are guards outside, so I'm going to go home and get some sleep. I know you're in good hands."

Matteo stood and shook his hand. Marcus came to the bed and crouched down. "I'm glad you're awake, Evie. He isn't right without you anymore, so get better and go back where you belong. Beside him—okay?"

"Okay," I whispered, my voice thick.

He left, and Matteo returned to the bed. He held my hand, stroking the bruised skin. He was quiet for a few moments, then he began to speak.

"I didn't know if I could get to you. I didn't know what I would find when I arrived. All I knew, the one thing I was certain of, was if you were gone, my life would cease to exist." He raised his eyes, and I was shocked at the tears that filled them. "You are my life, Evie. My everything. I'm done protecting the world. From this day forward, I will spend my life protecting you. Our family." A tear rolled down his face. "I will never risk you again. I cannot be without you."

He dropped his head, and his shoulders began to shake as he crumpled. I edged over, pulling on his arm, and he crawled onto the bed beside me. He had never allowed me to see him so vulnerable. I held him as best I could with the wires and bandages, marveling that this man was mine. That there was so much goodness under the darkness I had first seen. That he was capable of such love.

I pressed a kiss to his head and let my own tears flow. We could weep tonight and share our demons.

I vowed tomorrow was a new day—one without fear.

One we could face together.

EPILOGUE

Evie

Laughter and high-pitched giggles floated up from the beach, the sound making me smile. I walked to the edge of the deck, peering down at the open expanse. Matteo was tossing Maia in the air, with our twins, Anthony and Leo, clinging to Vince's legs as he crab-walked toward the water. Gianna came up beside me, her laughter quiet but happy.

"Look at them."

"I know." I sighed, contented. "They love having you here."

She slipped her arm around my shoulders and squeezed me affectionately. "We love it here too."

I watched my husband and daughter play in the sand. His head was bent over hers, the color of their hair so similar you couldn't tell where his ended and hers began. She was born here on this private island far off the grid, safe and secure. Born in the sun and warmth of the place that restored both Matteo and me. She brought the joy back into our world.

Gianna walked down the steps to the beach, and I sat down with a weary sigh. I felt tired today.

My thoughts drifted to the past.

We never returned to the house. When I left the hospital a week after I woke up, we boarded a private plane that took us thousands of miles away from the blood and pain of Matteo's past life.

The man the world knew as Matteo Campari and his wife Evie simply disappeared. His company was closed, the house sold, and rumors flew about their sudden departure. We didn't care. New papers, last names, and identifications rewrote the past, and we set out to create a different future. All that came with us were the small boxes of personal items Marcus and Matteo had packed and removed from the house.

For weeks, we strolled the sun-drenched beaches of the Mediterranean and healed together. It took Matteo a long time to relax, and I knew that, to some extent, he never would.

When Matteo found this group of islands, he knew we'd found our home. Large, private, and sprawling, it was still easy access to larger areas by boat or helicopter. It was a community of other people like us—those looking for a fresh start. No questions were asked, and we were welcomed graciously.

We settled into the villa, and not long after, Maia was born. I had never witnessed joy the way I did the day she arrived.

Matteo held her so carefully, the love spilling over from his eyes. He'd changed overnight. His smile was constant, his happiness contagious. Soon, the visitors started, and they became permanent residents. Vince and Gianna first, then Geo and Lila, and finally Alex and Roza. We all had our own villas and space—even our own lives, but the main beach was our shared playground.

Geo stayed busy, helping many people in the little area with medical issues, opening a small clinic on the main island. Lila helped him out there. Roza taught the younger children, and Alex and Vince ran a charter boat company. Gianna was still best in the safety of their home and continued to work behind the scenes on the monies the foundation issued. I helped her on occasion, but Matteo and my three children kept me occupied most of the time.

Marcus would be joining us soon. He had done his time heading up the team. He had finally found his own life and was ready to leave the old one behind. Matteo was certain once Julian decided to retire, he would head this way as well.

The team would have a new director and new members, still fighting against the underbelly of the world far too many became victim to, yet most people knew nothing about. It was, as Marcus often said, a never-ending battle.

After six years, Matteo proved to be true to his word. He was the fiercest of protectors, the most loving father, and the sexiest husband I could ask for. His eyes were clear and bright these days, the torment of his earlier life fading away with the years. He had his moments, but the sun and water always seem to wash them away.

And me. He said I was the brightest sunbeam in his life.

I startled as Matteo sat on the edge of my lounger, interrupting my musings. He smiled, the ends of his hair tinted gold from the sun, his skin darker than when I first met him. His brown eyes were warm as he leaned forward, pressing a lingering kiss to my mouth.

"Hello, my wife."

I smiled, running my hand along his short beard. He was barely recognizable from the man in the warehouse so many years ago.

"Hello, my husband."

"You looked very contemplative." He ran his hand over my rounded stomach. "Our girl causing you some discomfort?"

I covered his hand with mine. "No, I was just thinking."

"About?"

"When we got here."

He leaned forward, giving me another kiss. "Only good thoughts now, Evie. Those days are long past. We're all together and safe. Nothing is going to change that."

"Oh, I know." I hastened to assure him. "I was simply thinking how wonderful it is to have our whole family here."

"Soon, there will be one more."

I smiled. "Yes. Another daughter for you to spoil."

He grinned. "Maia is so excited about going to school next month. I'll miss her here every day. She has grown so fast. So have the boys."

I chuckled. "You're going to take her and Roza in the boat every day, Matteo, and pick her up. She'll only be gone a few hours. It will be good for her to have other children to play with."

"I know. I don't have to like it, though. She's my best little buddy." He shot me a teasing smirk. "We'll just have to keep having new ones so I don't get too lonely."

I shook my head in resignation. "Whatever you say."

He stood, lifting me in his arms. He kissed me, the caress long, lingering, and filled with promise. "I thought you'd see it my way. I think we should go practice a little. Gianna and Vince are taking the kids out on the boat, and the house is empty."

I smiled at him, cupping his cheek.

"Okay, Boss."

He threw back his head in laughter and strode into the house, his mouth hovering over mine.

"That's right, Evie. *I'm* the Boss." He winked. "As long as *you* say it's okay."

I joined in his laughter.

We both knew there would only ever be one true Boss.

And he was mine.

Thank you so much for reading THE BOSS. If you are so inclined, reviews are always welcome by me at your eretailer.

An additional thank you goes to all the members on Verve Romance who read the original serial and asked for more of Matteo and Evie.

Next in the series is a man of little words and made a impact in reader's minds - SECOND-IN-COMMAND.

If you would like to read more in romantic suspense, BENTLEY is an opposites attract with a heroine who is an even match for our hero.

Enjoy reading! Melanie

ACKNOWLEDGMENTS

Thank you to my wonderful readers who encouraged
me to write this book.
I hope you enjoyed it!

Lisa—the keeper of the red pen. How swiftly you use it
on my words.
You make them so much better. Thank you.
(you can go ahead and correct this now)

Beth, Trina, Melissa, Barbara, Sharon, and Deb—thank
you for your valuable input,
your keen eyes, and encouragement. Your humor and
help are so appreciated.

Karen—what you do for me daily as my PA is endless.
What you do for me as my friend is priceless.
Thank you for being on this journey with me.

Kim—for the work I thank you, for

the laughter and support, I treasure you. Thank you for your comments to make this a stronger story.

My reader group, Melanie's Minions—love you all.

Melanie's Literary Mob—my promo team—you do me proud and I love our interactions.
You are my happy place and I love sharing time with you.
Your support is amazing and humbling.

To all the bloggers, grammers, ticktok-y-ers. Thank you for everything you do. Shouting your love of books—of my work, posting, sharing—your recommendations keep my TBR list full, and the support you have shown me is deeply appreciated.

And my Matthew—you never complain when you lose me to another world. You encourage, support, and love.
I am the luckiest woman in the world
Because I have you.
Always.

ALSO AVAILABLE FROM MORELAND BOOKS

Titles published under M. Moreland

Insta-Spark Collection

It Started with a Kiss

Christmas Sugar

An Instant Connection

An Unexpected Gift

Harvest of Love

Titles published under Melanie Moreland

The Contract Series

The Contract (Contract #1)

The Baby Clause (Contract #2)

The Amendment (Contract #3)

Vested Interest Series

BAM - The Beginning (Prequel)

Bentley (Vested Interest #1)

Aiden (Vested Interest #2)

Maddox (Vested Interest #3)

Reid (Vested Interest #4)

Van (Vested Interest #5)

Halton (Vested Interest #6)

Sandy (Vested Interest #7)

Vested Interest/ABC Crossover

A Merry Vested Wedding

ABC Corp Series

My Saving Grace (Vested Interest: ABC Corp #1)

Finding Ronan's Heart (Vested Interest: ABC Corp #2)

Loved By Liam (Vested Interest: ABC Corp #3)

Age of Ava (Vested Interest: ABC Corp #4)

Men of Hidden Justice

The Boss

Second-In-Command

The Commander

Mission Cove

The Summer of Us

Standalones

Into the Storm

Beneath the Scars

Over the Fence

My Image of You (Republishing 2022)

Changing Roles

Happily Ever After Collection

Revved to the Maxx

Heart Strings

ABOUT THE AUTHOR

NYT/WSJ/USAT international bestselling author Melanie Moreland, lives a happy and content life in a quiet area of Ontario with her beloved husband of thirty-plus years and their rescue cat, Amber. Nothing means more to her than her friends and family, and she cherishes every moment spent with them.

While seriously addicted to coffee, and highly challenged with all things computer-related and technical, she relishes baking, cooking, and trying new recipes for people to sample. She loves to throw dinner parties, and enjoys traveling, here and abroad, but finds coming home is always the best part of any trip.

Melanie loves stories, especially paired with a good wine, and enjoys skydiving (free falling over a fleck of dust) extreme snowboarding (falling down stairs) and piloting her own helicopter (tripping over her own feet.) She's learned happily ever afters, even bumpy ones, are all in how you tell the story.

Melanie is represented by Flavia Viotti at Bookcase Literary Agency. For any questions regarding subsidiary or translation rights please contact her at flavia@bookcaseagency.com

Connect with Melanie

Like reader groups? Lots of fun and giveaways! Check it out Melanie Moreland's Minions

Join my newsletter for up-to-date news, sales, book announcements and excerpts (no spam). Click here to sign up Melanie Moreland's newsletter

or visit https://bit.ly/MMorelandNewsletter

Visit my website www.melaniemoreland.com

facebook.com/authormoreland

twitter.com/morelandmelanie

instagram.com/morelandmelanie

CPSIA information can be obtained
at www.ICGtesting.com
Printed in the USA
BVHW031616220622
640289BV00025B/1634